The Captive Princess

DAUGHTERS of the FAITH SERIES

The Captive Princess

A STORY BASED ON THE LIFE OF YOUNG POCAHONTAS

Wendy Lawton

MOODY PUBLISHERS
CHICAGO

All Scripture quotations are taken from the King James Version.

Published in association with the Books & Such Literary Agency, 52 Mission Circle, Suite 122, PMB 170, Santa Rosa, CA 95409-5370, www.booksandsuch.biz.

Editor: Cheryl Dunlop
Interior Design: Ragont Design
Cover Design: LeVan Fisher Design
Cover Images: indian girl © glenn morales/corbis
               fabric © Linda Webb/Shutterstock
               flower © Jupiterimages/Brand X/Corbis
               jamestown settlement reproduced courtesy of © Creative Commons

Library of Congress Cataloging-in-Publication Data

Lawton, Wendy.
    The captive princess : a story based on the life of young Pocahontas / by Wendy Lawton.
       p. cm. — (Daughters of the faith ; bk. 7)
    Includes bibliographical references and index.
    ISBN-10: 0-8024-7640-6
    ISBN-13: 978-0-8024-7640-1 (alk. paper)
    1. Pocahontas, d. 1617—Juvenile fiction. 2. Powhatan Indians—Juvenile fiction. 3. Indians of North America—Virginia—Juvenile fiction. I. Title.
PZ7.L4425 Ca 2008
[Fic]—dc22

                                                            2007039037

We hope you enjoy this book from Moody Publishers. Our goal is to provide high-quality, thought-provoking books and products that connect truth to your real needs and challenges. For more information on other books and products written and produced from a biblical perspective, go to www.moodypublishers.com or write to:

Moody Publishers
820 N. LaSalle Boulevard
Chicago, IL 60610

1 3 5 7 9 10 8 6 4 2

Printed in the United States of America

For Madeline and Miranda,
Twenty-first-century Daughters of the Faith

Contents

1

Setting the Captive Free

Shouts from the edge of the forest shattered the afternoon quiet. Pocahontas and Matachanna dropped the oyster shells they'd been using to scrape a deerskin pelt. Besides shouts, Pocahontas could pick out the howls and yelps of agitated dogs, along with the chattering of a frightened animal. As she stood craning her neck to get a better view, she saw an intent knot of boys and dogs. Furtive over-the-shoulder looks from the circle of boys told Pocahontas that something was afoot.

"Maraowanchesso!" Boys could be such nuisances. She pulled her sister to her feet. "Look at those boys over there—across the footbridge by the edge of the trees."

"I see." Matachanna squinted her eyes against the bright afternoon sun. "What are they doing?"

"I wish I knew." Pocahontas crept closer. "The way those dogs bark and circle, it must have to do with hunting."

"Where are the mothers?" Matachanna asked.

"They're preparing the ground for planting—too far away to hear. We'd best go see." Pocahontas pulled off the fur mantle she wore. It kept her warm on days like today, but she couldn't move as quickly in it.

Matachanna also removed hers. She folded it and put it beside the pelt frame.

Another round of yelping punctuated by chirpy cries sent the two girls hurrying toward the creek. Pocahontas made her way across the peeled log that bridged the creek first, followed by her younger sister.

The final snowmelt had swelled the creek, but neither girl feared water. Powhatan children swam as well as they walked. The mothers threw their children into water before they could even crawl. They claimed it hardened them off and made them strong. If the babies didn't enjoy the water so much, Pocahontas doubted the mothers would still do it, toughness or not. Powhatan parents loved their children.

Being a water baby had worked for Pocahontas. She could swim against the swiftest current if need be. Matachanna swam better than many of the boys her age, but she had a long way to go before she could match strokes with Pocahontas.

Of course the girls were just as agile traversing the footbridge, so swimming in the cold waters never entered Pocahontas's mind. She had nothing but the boys and their mischief on her mind.

One of the boys spotted the girls running toward them and called out a warning to his friends. The boys turned as one, their hands behind their backs. Standing shoulder to shoulder they faced the girls. They were hiding something.

The dogs continued to circle and bark.

"Hush," the oldest boy said. One of the dogs whined and quieted, but the rest ignored him.

"It's the princess," whispered another, his eyes widening.

Pocahontas pushed forward and the wall of boys opened for her. She smiled to herself. It never hurt to be the favored daughter of the most powerful man in all the land.

When she saw what caused the chaos, a familiar tightness gripped her chest. A large *arakun* wriggled against captivity, sputtering and chattering. His masked face registered anger and pain. He worked furiously with his nimble front paws to try to free his leg from the sinew bonds of the trap.

"We caught him in our trap," the first boy said. "He's just a 'rakun but a big one. A fighter."

"We captured him and he is our prisoner," said the littlest one.

Pocahontas knew she should be used to this. Young boys were supposed to learn to hunt. By the time of their *huskanaw*, their passage from boyhood to manhood, they were expected to be expert hunters. She understood that with her head, but her heart rebelled. For some reason, seeing a captive—whether animal or enemy—always made her uneasy.

She looked the oldest boy in the eye and pulled herself to her full height. "Let him go," she said in a voice that left no room for arguing.

Matachanna put a hand on Pocahontas's arm and whispered, "Are you sure?"

Pocahontas ignored her sister. "Let him go."

The oldest boy slid his wooden knife out of the leather thong around his waist. He sawed through the laces holding the animal.

When finally freed, the animal scurried toward the forest with dogs chasing him. Pocahontas knew the dogs would tree the animal but once up in the branches, the *arakun* would be safe.

She turned toward the boys. "You shall be great hunters someday, but never forget—a brave hunter kills his prey swiftly and painlessly. And he only takes what he needs to feed his people."

"Will you tell your father?" the oldest boy asked.

Pocahontas stood with her feet apart and put her hands on her hips. "My father would not like to hear that you were torturing the animal. *Arakun* is not our enemy." She could see worry on the faces of the boys. She smiled. "I will not tell the Powhatan."

As the boys ran off, probably to get into other mischief, Pocahontas sat on a fallen tree and turned toward Matachanna. "You tried to stop me, didn't you? I know you dislike it when I use my position to make people do what I want."

Her sister sat down next to her but didn't speak.

"I don't know why my father—our father—has bestowed such favor on me. I try to use my influence wisely." Pocahontas laughed. "Well, as wisely as I can, having seen only eleven returns of the new leaves."

"Of all our brothers and sisters, you are his favorite," Matachanna said. "He always says, 'My Matoaka, my Pocahontas, she it is who makes me smile.'" She drew out the words, deepening her voice.

Pocahontas laughed at her sister's impersonation of their great father. He spoke exactly like that. Her father began calling her Pocahontas—little mischief-maker—long before she could remember. Her real name was Amonute, though no one ever said that name. Many called her Matoaka, meaning little snow feather. But when her father started calling her Pocahontas, everyone else did as well.

She didn't really make mischief. It was her father's way of teasing her about walking on her hands instead of her feet, turning somersaults, and hanging from the tree limbs.

She thought about her father. Powerful. No other word described the great Powhatan as well. Her father accomplished what no other chief had ever accomplished. He united all the warring tribes into one great nation, Tsenacomoco. It took years of alliances, battles, and strategies, but here they were—at peace.

All the chiefs of those neighboring tribes gathered during *taquitock*, that time when the leaves turn colors, to bring tributes to the great Powhatan. Pocahontas loved to watch the canoes come ashore piled high with deerskins, *roanoke*, copper, corn, and puccoon root—all for her father. He built a storehouse almost as big as his ceremonial lodge to hold all the tributes.

"Does it seem unfair to you that our father favors me over all his children?" Pocahontas asked Matachanna. Sometimes it worried her. She had more than a hundred half-brothers and half-sisters, including Matachanna, and yet her father showed marked partiality only to her.

"I don't think so," Matachanna said, studying a beetle crawling on the side of her hand. "It has always been so for me."

Pocahontas loved this half-sister. Her father had many wives over his long life and many, many children. How glad she was that one of them turned out to be Matachanna. Her sister. Her friend.

"So you do not think I should have bullied the boys into letting the *arakun* go?"

Matachanna laughed. "I know you. You cannot stand to see anything held captive. I knew as soon as I saw that furry leg tangled in the trap that you would do whatever it took to save that *arakun*."

"You know me too well."

"I remember when the warriors brought Nokomias and her people to the village. You couldn't stop talking about that."

Pocahontas remembered as well.

In her tenth spring her father sent the braves of her village on a war party to massacre the Chesapeakes. Yes, her wise father, who had made peace with all other tribes—except the faraway Massawomecks, of course. She didn't like to think about the Chesapeakes. The entire time the warriors had been away, she did everything she could to keep from imagining what they were doing.

Even when she should have been sleeping, she thought about the Chesapeakes. She pictured war clubs, screams, and frightened children. Her heart pounded like a drum in her chest. She could feel the beat of it in her ears. When she woke with the morning sun and still could not put the scenes out of her mind, she made her way to her father's lodge, the largest building in the village. Several mats had been removed from the roof to let sunlight stream in, illuminating the great Powhatan. The rest of the lodge was dark and smelled of *apooke* smoke. Her father sat high on his platform of mats at the far end with his wise men crowded around him. Those warriors too old to join the raid stood around the perimeter of the room.

Pocahontas stood tall as she made her way to her father's dais and sat at his feet without speaking.

"I can see that you have a question dancing on your tongue, *amosens*." Her father used the word for daughter in front of all the men, signifying that he welcomed her. She knew that he always welcomed her, but many of his advisors did not approve of his favoritism. Besides being a child, she was a girl—to them it didn't make sense. The favorite should have been a son. Pocahontas had learned to ignore their frowns.

"Great Powhatan, I know that you rule with wisdom, but why have you sent our warriors out to battle the Chesapeake peoples?" Pocahontas knew this was a bold question and so she kept her voice respectful and formal.

"You always present difficult questions for me, don't you?" He smiled. "I knew you would be a match for me long ago when you were still a baby. The first words you spoke were questions." He reached down and touched her hair. "The ways of men and spirits are difficult to explain."

Pocahontas stayed silent.

"To forge this great nation, this Tsenacomoco, Okeus called us to fight and to make alliances. He told us to take lands and to take people. Yes, *amosens*, we had to take people. We needed to be ready to shoot an arrow into the heart of trouble before trouble could even notch his own arrow."

"But the Chesapeakes have been our friends."

"You speak truth. They always acted as friends, but our wise man—our *quiyoughsokuk*—received a powerful dream.

It told him that an invader would come from the land of the rising sun and that they would someday conquer our people." He took the *apooke* pipe between his lips, closed his eyes, and inhaled deeply. He handed the pipe off to the man seated to his left and let the smoke drift out his mouth. "How could the great Powhatan not answer that danger? Should I have let that threat to our people grow?"

"But are you sure it was the Chesapeakes?" Pocahontas wondered if the threat could have been the *Espaniuks* from across the waters.

Her father didn't answer. He folded his hands and closed his eyes—a sign that he refused to talk further about it.

It wasn't long afterward that the warriors finally came home and crowded into the great lodge. They were still painted for war, white ash slashed with black. They didn't even look like the men Pocahontas knew. She had been sitting on the dais near her father's feet, but when they began to regale their listeners with tales of slaughter and triumph, she stood to leave. As she walked toward the opening, she could see them dancing with the scalp locks. They raised them high in the air, giving whoops of triumph.

Pocahontas walked faster. She couldn't listen. She knew her father did not seek war recklessly and she knew his wisdom was greater than any other *weroance* who had ever served the Powhatan people, but she still could not bring herself to rejoice with her people over their victory.

The next day, a group of returning braves marched a handful of frightened Chesapeake women and children into Werowocomoco. Pocahontas's brother Nantaquaus returned with the warriors. As one of the favorite sons of the great

Powhatan, he held his head high, but Pocahontas noticed that he never met her eyes.

One boy they brought back from the Chesapeake raid had skin the color of the palest moon and hair that looked like corn silk. Strange. Pocahontas could not stop looking at him. Did his color mean he came from the water instead of the good red earth? Was he a different creature? No one would answer her questions. Finally her father told her that the boy went to live with the Arrohattoc. She wished she could have touched him.

One of the other children in the group was Nokomias.

⋱⋯ ⋱⋯ ⋱⋯ ⋱⋯

"Are you thinking about Nokomias?" Matachanna asked, bringing Pocahontas back to the present.

"I was remembering the day she came."

"Aren't you glad our village welcomes captives? Our father treats Nokomias like another daughter."

"But I don't understand why people must fight in the first place. If we hadn't wiped out the Chesapeakes, Nokomias would still be with her own people. No one would have had to adopt her."

Matachanna stood up. She had little patience for questioning.

"Why can't people live in peace?" Pocahontas had said those very words to herself many, many times. *Why can't we all live in peace?*

"Why do you ask so many questions, Pocahontas? It is

our way. It has always been our way. Our father says we fight so we can have peace at last."

Matachanna would never understand. She accepted things without question. "Come. Let's go back into the village and find Nokomias." Pocahontas crouched as if to push off for a faster start. "I'll race you to the footbridge."

"As if I could ever beat you in a footrace." The words were flung back at the crouching Pocahontas as Matachanna took off. She may have had a head start but Pocahontas would still beat her.

2

Werowocomoco

Pocahontas, Matachanna, and Nokomias worked side by side, each bending over a different row. They stayed close enough to talk but far enough apart to keep from bumping into one another.

"Shall we make it a competition?" Pocahontas asked.

"With you being the oldest and fastest, I wonder why you would suggest a contest?" Matachanna didn't smile, but Pocahontas knew she was being teased again. Matachanna was one of the few people in the village who ever dared to tease her.

Because of her powerful father, people often either treated her with excessive respect or else they were timid and hesitant. Pocahontas worked hard to overcome this by trying to be natural with people—by joking and teasing everyone into friendship. Nantaquaus once observed that her funny songs, somersaults, and antics were her way of trying to put people at ease. He probably wasn't far wrong.

"I don't want to race," Nokomias said. "This is my first

time to help with planting and I want to do it right. I have to keep repeating, 'Two bean, two squash, three corn; two bean, two squash, three corn.'"

"We ought to make up a song to help us." Matachanna loved to sing. She started to hum a tune.

"It would work except you both keep talking and before I realize it, I've planted three squash, two corn, and three bean." Nokomias sighed.

Pocahontas laughed at her friend. It hadn't been that long since Nokomias came to Werowocomoco. At first she seemed like one who walked in her sleep, but Pocahontas kept talking to her and including her whenever she and Matachanna played. Before long Nokomias began to talk a little. Never about her village or her people, but about whatever they were doing.

It was a start.

Recently, she had even begun to laugh once in a while. One of the mothers, Alaqua, had made a home for Nokomias in her lodge. Pocahontas was glad Nokomias had a new mother to watch over her.

"Why do we plant three kinds of seeds all together?" Nokomias asked. "In my village we planted the corn in one plot, squash in a different plot, and beans in yet another."

Matachanna looked at Pocahontas. That was the first time Nokomias had mentioned her village. Pocahontas recognized it as a big step.

"We plant them all together because the corn grows strong and tall and makes a pole for the beans to climb. The squash grows fast and broad, shading the tender shoots and keeping the earth moist." Pocahontas put another seed into the furrow.

"And there's something about planting them together that feeds the earth," Matachanna said. "Before we planted them together the mothers say we had to move our fields more often. Now they all grow stronger."

"So why do you plant two squash seeds, two beans, and three corn? Why not just one of each?"

"You ask almost as many questions as Pocahontas," Matachanna said.

Pocahontas pitched a soft clod of dirt toward her sister's head.

"Ouch!" Matachanna picked up a clod of her own and weighted it in her hand for a moment before letting it fall back to the ground. "We plant two beans, two squash seeds, and two kernels of corn to give the earth one for growing and another one to keep if she desires. If earth decides to send both shoots, we pluck the weaker one out of the ground to make room for the strong one." She stooped down and laid the seeds into another furrow.

"And we add the third kernel of corn because no matter how hard we work to keep the crows away, they always seem to steal at least one of the kernels of corn." Pocahontas eyed her sister moving ahead and increased her own rhythm. *Two bean, two squash, three corn; two bean, two squash, three corn . . .*

They did work hard to keep the crows away from the fields. In the middle of the field stood a platform called the scarecrow hut. The young boys took turns in the hut, scaring off the crows. They flapped their arms, danced, shouted, jumped, and even threw pebbles. Despite the ruckus, the determined crows still managed to dine on corn kernels.

"Why don't we push the earth over the seeds after putting

them in the furrow? It would save us having to come back to cover them," Nokomias asked.

"That's where the real secret comes," Pocahontas said. "See those mothers with baskets by the river?"

Nokomias shaded her eyes and looked toward the river.

"They are waiting for the boys to fill the baskets with fish from the nets," Pocahontas said.

"Yes. They'll come behind us and put a small fish in the furrow with the seeds and then cover the earth over the fish and seeds." Matachanna continued working down the row.

"A fish?" Nokomias looked confused. "What grows out of a fish? More fish?"

Pocahontas and her sister looked at their friend to see if she were teasing, but when they saw that she was serious, they both burst into laughter.

"The fish does not sprout like a seed," Pocahontas said as she kept laughing, pacing her words between gulps of air.

Matachanna interrupted so Pocahontas could catch her breath. "The fish rots in the ground and becomes food for the corn, squash, and beans."

Nokomias couldn't help laughing as well. "Everything is so strange here in Werowocomoco, I would not be surprised to see fish bushes growing right up with the other."

"Now that would be fun," Pocahontas said. "Can't you see the fish wriggling to get plucked off the vine and thrown into the river?"

The girls continued to laugh and talk as they finished all the rows for the first planting. During spring and *nepinough*, they planted three different times. That meant that there were three different times of harvest as well. They usually picked corn all through the summer.

This year, however, the mothers kept looking at the sky. "Where is the rain?" they whispered over and over.

Every morning the women woke early to spread a circle of *apooke*. They stood inside the circle to greet the sun, hoping to appease whatever god had decided to withhold rain from Werowocomoco. Without rain it was a tedious job to go down to the river and bring water in clay pots to water the seedlings, but if they didn't keep them moist, a starving time would come upon their people.

Each day when the girls finished their hard work, they played just as hard. Sometimes they swam or fished. Sometimes they just dug their toes into the sand at river's edge and talked. Other times Pocahontas took the lead and had them turning cartwheels and jumping from rock to rock. She had learned to flip her body in the air without using hands. Every time the other girls tried this, they landed flat on the ground. Wherever the three went, laughter followed.

It was unusual to see the three of them sitting quietly, but on a warm morning several days after the planting was finished Pocahontas took the basket of *roanoke* beads she'd been saving and divided them into three piles so each of them could fashion a new necklace onto *pemmenaw* thread. Their people wore many necklaces. Pocahontas loved to wear all of hers at one time and hear the click, click, click of beads as she walked.

"Wait," Nokomias said. "I have something for our necklaces." She ran toward her lodge and within minutes came back with a small leather pouch.

She took out three blue beads, handing one to Pocahontas, one to Matachanna, and putting the third on her pile of *roanoke*.

Pocahontas had never seen anything like it. She held it up to the sun. She turned it over in her hand. It was smooth and cool to the touch. She thought it looked like a small cylinder of water with a hole lengthwise through the center for the thread to pass through. "*Waugh*! This is beautiful. Where did you get it?"

"Did you see the boy, Micah? The one with yellow hair?" Nokomias paused as the girls nodded. "He came with some of his people to shelter with us."

"From what tribe?" Pocahontas asked. She'd never seen any people who looked like the boy.

"Not a tribe. They came from across the Great Water. From the land toward the rising sun." The girl shook her head. "They came and brought tools, copper, and beads like this, but they brought no food."

"Did they plant corn?" Matachanna asked.

"Not right away. And when they began to plant, most of the people were already sick and starving. Only a bit of the corn grew. Bald spots covered much of the field. Those ears that formed came too late."

"How did they come to be with you? How did you get these beads? Where is the boy's mother?" Pocahontas stopped. Nokomias did not often talk of her village. Pocahontas had as many questions as the *apasoum* has babies, but if she persisted, would her friend stop talking?

"Our people took the last of the strangers into our village to keep them from dying. Micah's mother became my friend. I helped her learn our language and she helped me learn some of hers."

Pocahontas wanted to hear the faraway language. Later she'd make sure Nokomias taught her words from the strangers.

"When I showed her how we tan hides and make clothing she gave me these beads." Nokomias picked up her bead. "She called them 'glass.'"

"It is beautiful." Pocahontas kept turning her bead to see how the sun made sparkles on it.

"You are my friends. I want you to share this gift from my friend Anna."

Pocahontas didn't ask what happened to Anna.

"Thank you," Matachanna said. "It will make the prettiest necklace of all."

"You honor us with this gift." Pocahontas's hand closed around her treasure. She would string this bead-like-water onto her necklace. She would remember Anna and Nokomias forever.

"If you help me finish my canoe, I will take you for a long trip, out toward the Great Water." Nantaquaus, Pocahontas's brother, had walked over to the center of the village to find the girls. Nokomias had been weeding the cornfield with Pocahontas and Matachanna, but he hung back as he spoke.

"Yes, we'll help you," Pocahontas said, including all three of them with a sweep of her hand. "You do the burning and we'll do the scraping."

"You go. I need to get back to Alaqua," Nokomias said, backing toward the village.

Pocahontas could see a look of understanding come over Nantaquaus's face.

"Wait, Nokomias," Nantaquaus said in a gentle voice. "Sit here." He pointed to a rise of soft grass.

Nokomias lowered her head but did as he asked. She hunched her shoulders and crossed her hands in her lap. The other two girls sat near her. Nantaquaus sat down as well, folding his legs and grasping his moccasin-covered feet.

"Nokomias, I forget you are a captive in our village. I forget that you witnessed what our warriors did to your people. I come and I ask you to help like a little sister, but I forget."

Nantaquaus's directness surprised Pocahontas. In all the time she and Nokomias had been friends, she'd been careful not to mention the massacre of her village. She didn't think of her as a captive anymore. She'd already become part of their village.

Nokomias didn't speak. Neither did Pocahontas or Matachanna.

"When you back away from me, I understand. You are remembering me that day at your village." Nantaquaus paused.

Nokomias kept her head lowered.

"Our great Powhatan, my father, sent us to rid our nation of a threat. As we obeyed those orders, we did not think of our brothers, the Chesapeakes. But on the march back to our village, I thought of little else. I had long hours to watch the faces of our captive women and children."

Nantaquaus's words surprised Pocahontas. Maybe she was not the only one who hated fighting.

Nokomias looked up at Nantaquaus.

"I am a warrior. I am the son of my father. A warrior begs not for mercy from a captive." He stood up, pulling his young body to its full height. As he started to walk away, he heard Nokomias's voice.

"I will help you." She said it in a whisper, but her words were clear.

Nothing more was said. The girls followed him to the river's edge where he had banked the dugout canoe he was finishing. He had chosen the trunk from a tall, straight cypress tree for the canoe. To hollow it, he had spent many days burning the inside. It took a long time because the heart of the trunk was still damp with life. The fire needed to be carefully tended so that it only consumed what Nantaquaus wanted it to consume.

"You are almost finished," Pocahontas said. Both ends of the *quintans*, the canoe, were rounded so it could glide through the waters. Nantaquaus had worked pitch onto the outside of his canoe to make it waterproof. The inside only needed the finish scraping to make it smooth and remove the last of the charred wood.

The girls took the scraping tools made of sharp oyster shells and went to work. They scraped and talked and laughed. The hours sped by. When they finished, Nantaquaus looked it over. "It is good." He smiled and walked around it again and again. "Tomorrow we take it on its very first journey."

Pocahontas went toward her sleeping lodge to find Matachanna's mother. Her own mother had died when she was small, so the other mothers cared for her—mostly Matachanna's mother.

She found her outside, grinding corn with some of the other women. "Tomorrow we plan to join my brother as he takes out his new canoe," Pocahontas said. "He invited Matachanna and Nokomias to come."

"Where will you go?" the mother asked.

Pocahontas knew the mothers would want to know where they were going and how long they would be gone, but she didn't need to ask for permission because children in their village were given freedom to explore as long as their work was finished.

"We will go down the river until we reach the mouth near the Great Water."

"You must take food for the journey," Alaqua said. "I will put some *ponepone* in a basket and some dried *weghshaughes*. You can pick berries on the way."

Pocahontas could barely sleep that night. As the moon rose above the village, she watched it through the opening in the roof matting of her sleeping lodge. Matachanna's regular breathing told her that her sister had no trouble sleeping.

How beautiful the moon looked. She thought about the stories her people told about how the *Gitchee Manitou*—the Great Spirit—created the moon. When He finished He spoke the words, "It is good." He was right. It was very good.

Gitchee Manitou, I wish I knew You. I have so many questions to ask You. You are the Father of all people, and You are more powerful than the great Powhatan. I want to know You like I know my father.

Something stirred within her. Maybe it was because she was excited about going with Nantaquaus to the very edge of land. Maybe not—but she sensed she was on the brink of something important.

A change.

As sleep began to wrap around her like a warm mantle, a whisper drifted into her dream, "*Amosens*, I have given you a heart to know Me. Search your heart."

3
Great White Bird

"This canoe slices through the water like an arrow through the sky." Nantaquaus stopped rowing to appreciate his new canoe. He ran his hand along the rim and smiled.

Their adventure began long before the sun rose to greet the day. They had packed their food into the canoe and decided where each would sit. As Nantaquaus pushed off, Pocahontas saw his chest fill with pride.

The air warmed as soon as the sun rose, and Pocahontas could see that it would be a perfect day. As they paddled downriver, they watched a beaver dive under the clear water to hide in his lodge of sticks. Shy foxes stood at the water's edge to drink but bolted back into the brush when they saw the canoe. Deer came out of the forest trailing speckled fawns. Fruit trees bloomed and wildflowers covered the riverbanks.

Nokomias breathed in deeply. "The air smells like flowers."

It did. The splash of the oars and the sound of the boat cutting through the water had a rhythmic, almost hypnotic feel. Bickering crows, the screech of an eagle, and the rat-tat-tat of a woodpecker punctuated the quiet.

"We're getting very near my old village," Nokomias said.

"Do you ever feel like running away, trying to go back to your village?" Matachanna asked.

Nantaquaus looked at Pocahontas. She understood what his eyes communicated. There was no village to go back to.

"No," Nokomias said. "My family is gone and my village . . . well, who knows." She sat silently for a while. "When I came to Werowocomoco, I tried to stay busy with my hands so my mind and my heart had no time to think or to feel. Eventually, instead of feeling sad, I became angry. I felt like a captive. I used to think about ways to escape."

Pocahontas could imagine what that kind of anger could do. She didn't even want to think about how she'd feel if her family had been killed.

"After I came to live with Alaqua and became friends with you and Pocahontas, the anger faded. I don't feel like a captive anymore. I have nowhere to go. You are now my people."

It seemed strange to Pocahontas that a person could come to accept the very people who had captured her.

Nantaquaus steered the canoe into a side creek. "Shall we eat? I saw berry bushes over there." He pointed to a thicket. "It might be early for gooseberries, but strawberries shouldn't be hard to find."

The girls took the baskets they brought for berry picking and fanned out. It didn't take long until they each had a basketful.

Though they never saw any other people, they knew the

clearing must have been made by the Chiskiack. All the land had been forested until cleared by people. If a clearing were abandoned it was because the tribe had moved on to let that piece of land rest. They would come back and plant it again when fertility had been restored. They knew that, no matter where they stepped, the land belonged to one tribe or another, even if nobody cultivated it at that time. For as far as a man could paddle in three days, in any direction, all the land belonged to tribes loyal to Powhatan.

"Are you ready to continue?" Nantaquaus asked.

"Yes," Pocahontas said. "I want to see the Great Water."

They settled into the canoe and began paddling again. As the river grew wider and wider, she realized that they had entered the bay.

"This is the Chesapeake," Nantaquaus said, glancing toward Nokomias.

"I remember," she said. "The scent brings it back even more strongly."

Pocahontas leaned forward to put an arm around her friend.

"If we keep on going, we'll be on the Great—" Nantaquaus stopped speaking mid-sentence and put his hand up for silence.

There, far out toward the direction of the Great Water, sat what looked like three great white birds perched on the water. Pocahontas blinked. They couldn't be birds. They were bigger than Powhatan's ceremonial lodge.

Nantaquaus used every muscle in his body to silently paddle the canoe to the shore. He beached the canoe in a copse of trees and motioned for the girls to get out.

"We need to understand what we see so we can report to our father," he whispered.

Whatever it was, it was far enough away so that their voices wouldn't carry. The wind was blowing from the Great Water toward them, so it was even less likely that sound or scent would carry to whatever rested on the water.

They hid the canoe in a tangle of branches and Nantaquaus signaled for them to follow him.

"Are you afraid?" Matachanna asked Pocahontas.

"Not afraid. More curious than afraid."

"Take damp earth and rub it on your skin so our faces will be less likely to be seen." Nantaquaus reached down for a handful of mud and began smearing it across his face and chest. "Stay in the trees and make sure you are covered."

As they topped the rise, Pocahontas could see that the objects were not birds. A shiver touched her back. They were more like *quintansuk*—giant boats, but not like any she'd ever seen.

"Do you see what they are?" she asked Nantaquaus.

He nodded.

"I think I know what we see," Nokomias said. "Anna described them to me. They are what she called 'sailing ships.' They come from across the Great Water where there is another land as big as our land."

"Sailing ships?" Pocahontas wanted to say the word over and over until she got it right. "Sailing ships."

"We need to see what manner of men come on these 'sailing ships,'" Nantaquaus said. "Are they warriors?"

As the ships came closer, they could see movement under the wings. The creatures had shells like the turtle—shells that glinted in the sun.

"Are they men or animals?" Pocahontas asked. "Those two I can make out have fur on their faces like animals. But they walk like men."

"Stay down, Pocahontas. We don't want them to see us." Nantaquaus motioned for all of them to come in closer. The underbrush had not been burned, so that made it easier to hide.

"Those . . . how did you say it, Nokomias?" Pocahontas turned to her friend. "Ships?"

Nokomias nodded.

"Those ships must still be far away because the people look so small."

Nantaquaus agreed. "They are still in the Great Water but they are coming this way. The wind is behind their white wings, pushing them into the Chesapeake."

Matachanna had been quiet as she watched. "I want to go back to our village."

"Matachanna's right. We need to go back and tell our father what we've seen," Nantaquaus said.

"But don't we want to watch longer so we can tell him more about them?" Pocahontas asked. She longed to stay. "I know we can stay hidden."

Matachanna and Nokomias grasped hands. Pocahontas could sense their fear.

"No, we must leave," Nantaquaus said. "The trip back will be slower since we must paddle against the current."

"How do we keep from being seen by them?" Matachanna asked.

"They are still far enough away that we will not be easily seen. We will keep toward the shore where the bends in the river should hide us until we are out of sight," Nantaquaus said.

Pocahontas thought of something else that made her laugh. "We were perfectly created for hiding. Look at our skin, the color of earth. Look at our clothing, the color of the deer. Look at our hair, the color of the depths of the river. Even Nantaquaus's canoe is the color of the forest."

Nantaquaus laughed with her. "You have good eyes to see, little sister. I never thought of that. The *Gitchee Manitou* made us like the deer. He blends into the forest so well that if he did not move you might not see him."

"I wonder if the bird canoes come from a land of snow and ice?" Matachanna asked. "Their ship is white, their faces are pale, and their clothing shines like sun on ice."

"My friend Anna had a pale face and pale hair and when she talked about her land—England, she called it—she didn't talk about snow and ice."

"England. England," Pocahontas repeated. "That's the land you said lies across the Great Water?"

"Yes."

Nantaquaus began to make his way back to the canoe. He put a hand over his mouth to remind them to stay quiet.

"I wonder if it is the same as the land of the *Espaniuks*?" Pocahontas had heard the wise men talk about the much-feared *Espaniuks*.

"No," Nokomias said. "I remember Anna saying that the *Espaniuks* were enemies of her people. She said they were— what was the word? I think it was pirates."

"Pirates. Pirates. What does that word mean?" Pocahontas

now had three *tassantassa* words: sailing ship, England, and pirates.

"I think they are raiders. She talked about them stopping the boats on the Great Water, killing the people or taking them captive, and taking the boat and weapons."

"If these white bird ships are enemies of the *Espaniuk*, our father may welcome them."

As they paddled away, the great white birds became smaller and smaller until they could no longer be seen.

Pocahontas stayed silent as she helped paddle against the current, but she couldn't keep from thinking about what they had just seen. Maybe it was because of her dream last night, but she sensed that the change she had felt coming had arrived. Why was she so sure it had arrived on those three white bird ships?

As their tired group got closer to Werowocomoco, she felt certain that her life would never be the same again. She couldn't say why, but she knew.

4

Tassantassuk

When the tired group finally made it back to Werowoco-moco, Matachanna and Nokomias went to their sleeping lodges. It had been a long day.

Nantaquaus and Pocahontas agreed to meet after they bathed. They'd go to Powhatan's lodge together.

Pocahontas washed her hair and dried it on a bunch of turkey feathers. The feathers absorbed water, but they also made her long hair shiny. She separated the hair into three portions and braided it, weaving in a turkey feather to make it prettier. She put on all her necklaces, including the new one with Anna's blue bead. She strung the pearls that her father had given her into the holes of her earlobes. She loved the feel of the pearls bumping against her neck as she moved.

She tied a fresh deerskin apron around her waist and set the one she wore earlier across a sassafras bush to sweeten.

She tried to hurry because she knew Nantaquaus would not take as much time. She always teased him that it only took him half the time because he only wore half the clothes and had half the hair. Warriors in her village shaved the right half of their heads. She had always thought it was just to make them look more handsome, but her brother laughed when she said that.

"We scrape the hair off so that it won't get tangled in our bowstrings," he had said.

It made sense. So much of what they did to decorate themselves had a purpose. Sometimes it was a practical purpose like shaving half a head or bathing often to remove human scent, which could be detected by animals and enemies. Other beauty rituals were to bond the people together, like the tattoos.

Pocahontas remembered when she was tattooed. The mother who did it was a great artist. She took a thorn and pricked tiny holes all the way around Pocahontas's upper arm. The pain was great and lasted for what seemed like a very long time, but she remained silent. She didn't want word to reach her great father that she had acted like a baby. After every few prickings, the mother dropped paint made from puccoon root and hazelnut oil onto the wound.

When it was finally finished, Pocahontas couldn't wait to jump into the cold creek to numb the pain. Just as she stood up to go, the mother told her not to get it wet. She needed to let it soak into her flesh. It throbbed the night through, but in the morning Pocahontas removed the medicine leaves and was surprised to see a delicate tracery of vines and leaves with tiny dots for berries. One poke after another and this beautiful design resulted.

As she left her lodge, she saw Nantaquaus walking toward her.

"Good. You dressed to honor our father. We have important information to give him. We may have to answer questions from many of his advisors."

As they walked across the village and crossed the ditches that marked the area set off for the Powhatan, Pocahontas thought about delivering the news. Normally, she used smiles and somersaults to soften bad news. The mothers always said there was no one who could tease them out of a bad humor quicker than Pocahontas. From the time she could first walk, she remembered watching faces. She had been given the gift of knowing how to approach people. Some people responded to her antics with smiles and laughter, and other people responded to her serious side. She took pride in the fact that everyone in the village seemed to like her. And not only because her father favored her—she worked hard to earn their friendship and respect.

Sometimes her brother teased her because he knew she liked being smart and funny. He would say that people didn't like her for those reasons; they only liked her because she was the prettiest girl in Werowocomoco. He knew this displeased her, so he teased her all the more.

Most said she was beautiful, tall and straight with keen eyes and a ready smile. But beauty was not something that should ever make a difference. You could not help your stature or your face, but you could help how you treated people.

Nobody liked a show-off. Pocahontas knew this. Like the young brave from a nearby village who wore a small writhing snake through his ear piercing. He strutted, just waiting for people to notice him. Did anyone think about what it was like for that baby snake to have to go about poked through an ear piercing all day?

No. Beauty was no reason to be honored.

"You're quiet," Nantaquaus said.

"I'm wondering how they will take the report. I'm hoping they won't send out war parties to fight the *tassantassuk*."

"Why?"

"I don't know. Wouldn't it be better to learn to know them? I want to know their strange language. I'd like to know about their land."

Nantaquaus laughed. "You don't want us to shoot them with arrows because you want to torture them to death with your questions."

Pocahontas pinched him. "Tell me you don't wish to know how they make those white birds that float on water?"

Nantaquaus folded his arms across his chest.

"And do you not wish to touch the clothing that reflects the sun?"

"Your curiosity may be dangerous, little sister. Come, let us go in and speak to our father."

The sun had gone down and the lodge was darker and smokier than usual. The fire cast eerie shadows on the faces of the men around Powhatan.

As Pocahontas and Nantaquaus made their way down the long hall they could see that the galleries on either side were filled with men from their village along with a few visitors from nearby villages.

Nantaquaus turned back to look at Pocahontas. She knew what his look meant—stick by me, we are intruding here.

Powhatan would not embarrass her for intruding on a meeting or ceremony, but he was much tougher on Nantaquaus.

When they got to the platform where Powhatan sat, Nantaquaus bowed low and then stepped back toward the side until his father was ready to acknowledge him. Pocahontas sat down near his feet on the edge of the dais.

As Powhatan reached out to touch her hair, she could see her uncle Opechancanough stiffen. He made no attempt to hide his irritation at having a girl in their meeting.

"So daughter, why do you come to me so long after the sun has set? Surely you do not wish to tell me about your trip today."

"Great Powhatan, we wish to tell you and your wise council about the strange things we saw."

Opechancanough crossed his arms across his chest and schooled his face into a look of exaggerated impatience. Pocahontas knew that their news would quickly wipe that look off his face.

"Nantaquaus, come forward." Powhatan leaned forward. The fur and feathers on his headdress quivered. "Tell me what you saw."

And Nantaquaus did.

Pocahontas watched the faces of her father, her uncle, and the other men. They went from indifference to skepticism to intense interest.

"These ships," Opechancanough interrupted. "Do you think they carry *Espaniuks*?"

"I do not know," Nantaquaus answered. He'd never seen *Espaniuks*.

"You did well, children," Powhatan said. "You watched

without being seen. You discovered much about them and brought the information directly to me. Well done."

Pocahontas stood to leave. Her father reached out to touch her cheek. "Do not be afraid, Matoaka. We will deal with these *tassantassuk* on our shore."

Pocahontas smiled. She hadn't been afraid. She was mostly curious. All she knew was that she wanted to know everything about these strangers. She hoped they would eventually meet.

⁂

Questions. Pocahontas always had questions, but ever since seeing the sailing ships of the *tassantassuk*, she had more questions than ever and almost no way to seek answers. Who were they? What did they want? Did they plan to stay? What were they like?

When she heard that an envoy from the Paspahegh chief, Wowinchopunck, came to report to her father about a meeting with the strangers, Pocahontas slipped into the meeting lodge and made her way to her familiar perch at the feet of her father.

They were midway into the report when she arrived. "The *tassantassuk* are camping on Paspahegh ground, near the Chesapeake bay," the envoy said.

"But that land is swamp land," Powhatan said. "There's no fresh water from the Pamunkey River to the Powhatan River. That's why your tribe abandoned it as a good place for a village."

"Yes, but that is where they have settled," the envoy said.

Powhatan nodded his head up and down slowly and turned to his advisors. "This is good. It either means they do not plan to stay long or it means they are fools. Either way, they will not trouble us for long."

"But they do not sleep on their great canoes like men who only explore. They cut down trees to build shelters, and they've begun to build a wall around their village."

"A wall? Like we build our lodges with frames and grass mats?" Powhatan cocked his head. Pocahontas knew that gesture. He was trying to picture it.

"No. They take one tree and bury it in the ground pointing toward the sky. Then they take the next tree, drive it into the ground right next to it, and use crosspieces to connect the logs together. Many, many trees, all standing, form the wall."

Pocahontas did not understand why they would build these walls. How she wished her father would ask why.

"They came to us to buy food." The visitor set a basket in front of Powhatan with bits of copper, beads, and some metal knives.

Powhatan examined each piece, especially the copper. The last copper they'd traded for all those years ago had been used, and there was little they prized more highly for making jewelry than this metal. Pocahontas fingered the copper disk strung on her necklace.

"We bring these for you, great Powhatan," the man said.

Powhatan pressed his hands on his chest in thanks for the tribute. He lifted the knife out of the basket and felt the blade. "Good weapon."

"Yes, but it is their firesticks that carry real magic."

"Firesticks?"

"Yes, hollow sticks that spit fire and pebbles as far as an arrow can travel or even farther. We saw them when Wowinchopunck led a party of nearly one hundred braves to their settlement to welcome them."

Pocahontas smiled. She knew that the visit was as much because of curiosity as it was out of welcome.

The man went on, "We brought them a deer as a gift. One of our men picked up a hatchet that had been discarded on the ground. As he walked away, a *tassantassa* lifted his firestick and shot, killing him instantly."

"Can you bring me one of those firesticks?" Powhatan asked.

"No, they won't trade for them and they never let them out of their hands."

"Maybe I will have to see these *tassantassa* myself," Powhatan said, half to himself.

"Our chief wishes to know how you want us to deal with these strangers. Are they friends or are they enemies?"

Powhatan paused for a time, stroking the strands of pearls around his neck, before speaking. "Let me have some of our women bring you food. Sit outside and rest while I talk to my advisors."

After the man left, Pocahontas tried to keep from making the slightest movement. If she stayed still and silent, perhaps her father wouldn't ask her to leave.

"I think we should assemble a war party and rid our nation of this danger," Opechancanough said.

"Do we know they are a danger?" Powhatan said. "With their firesticks, if they became allies, we could finally conquer our one last enemy—the tribes of the Iroquois nation. Maybe we should watch them to see what they do."

"So, do we instruct our allied tribes to treat them as friends?" the oldest adviser, Powhatan's brother Rawhunt, asked.

"No, we do not know if they are friends or enemies. We need to know more about these *tassantassuk*."

"I think we should strike," Opechancanough said. "But if you plan to discover more about them, how will you do that?"

Powhatan stayed silent for a long time before speaking. "I will send word to each tribe to deal with *tassantassuk* as they see fit. They can treat them like friends or they can treat them like enemies. We will ask to receive reports of every contact. We will only learn about these strangers by watching how they respond."

Pocahontas planned to be there to hear every report. She, too, wanted to discover more about them.

5

Friends or Enemies

Nearly every day since the *tassantassuk* arrived in their great white sailing birds, envoys came to Powhatan to report on their strange doings. Pocahontas hurried to Powhatan's lodge every time a visitor came to Werowocomoco to speak to her father.

"We do not understand," one Arrohattoc envoy reported. "They come to our village and we prepare a feast of venison, corn, beans, cakes, and mulberries. We talk with them, trying to help them understand our village and our allegiance to the great Powhatan. We tell them you are the *Mamanatowic*."

Pocahontas's father bowed his head to acknowledge the truth of that tribute.

"We trade food to them for knives and beads—a fair trade. They keep asking more questions about our 'king.'" The man gestured with an open hand toward Powhatan. "This is how they speak of you."

"King." Powhatan tried the word. "King."

"They do not speak our language well. Their understanding is limited. We decide to send Nauiraus with them to learn their tongue."

Powhatan smiled and nodded. "And, of course, you knew that Nauiraus could tell you more about what they did and where they went."

Pocahontas knew that her father always considered the strategy behind every decision.

The man smiled and continued, "During their visit we receive word that Parahunt will join us for a meal."

Parahunt was one of Pocahontas's older half-brothers but she barely knew him. He'd been living in a different village as chief for as long as she could remember. The few times she'd seen him, he ignored her, paying attention only to their great father.

"Our *weroance* tries to tell the *tassantassuk* that Parahunt is your son and he is chief at the village of Powhatan. They do not understand that though you are called Powhatan, our people are also called Powhatan—all our people and all our tribes—and we have a village called Powhatan."

It didn't surprise Pocahontas that they mixed that up. She often wondered why her people didn't use different names.

"They mistake Parahunt for you, Powhatan," the man said. "They give him gifts of many knives, beads, copper, and tools. Even the women laugh at the mistake."

Pocahontas could see by the way her father rubbed his hand over his face that he wondered why Parahunt hadn't reported to him and brought the proper portion of the treasure as a tribute. It didn't matter that Parahunt was his son; her father was the ruler of all and one did not slight him.

When the envoy had eaten and left, Powhatan discussed what he'd heard with his advisors. "These *tassantassuk* know nothing of our people. They meet the Paspahegh and receive friendship at their hands. Without understanding, they go next to the Arrohattoc, the enemies of the Paspahegh. Who is to trust them?"

All the advisors laughed and made mocking comments.

Pocahontas wondered how *tassantassuk* were supposed to know which tribes were allies and which were enemies. Besides, you might even be a friendly tribe, like the Chesapeakes, and still find yourself facing a wall of warriors. Just because her father's advisors understood the complicated politics of their nation didn't mean an outsider could sort it out.

All she knew was that she longed to find out for herself about these *tassantassuk*. She needed to have her questions answered and she wanted to judge for herself.

"There are grasses outside their village tall enough to hide a man," Nantaquaus said as he paddled his canoe down the Pamunkey River. Early this morning Pocahontas finally talked him into going with her to get a look at the *tassantassuk* village.

"Why do they not cut the grasses if the weeds are tall enough to shield a war party?" Pocahontas asked. "Anyone could attack without being seen."

"No one knows why they do such strange things. But you should be glad they leave the grasses; otherwise I never would have agreed to take you."

"They do so many strange things, according to the reports. Like digging in the ground all the time for something they call gold. Why would they spend so much time digging on barren hillsides when they haven't planted their corn?" Pocahontas shook her head. "Do you think gold is some kind of food we don't know about?"

"How many questions are you going to ask, little sister, before you give me a chance to answer one?" Nantaquaus slapped the water with his oar, splashing her with a spray of water. "Our father thinks this gold they seek is a rock that their people value like we value *roanoke*."

Pocahontas thought about that. "Everyone thinks them fools but I think they are just different from us. Our people want to know what they do and where they go. I want to know why they do what they do and why they go where they go."

"If you were a bird your single song would be why-why-why."

"Don't you ever wonder why?"

"Being around you makes me wonder about the whys," Nantaquaus said. "It's probably not a good thing for a warrior to be wondering. A warrior needs to be quick on his feet and willing to follow his leader—not ask questions."

"But if you become a *weroance* or even *Mamanatowic*, searching for answers would be very good, would it not?"

"You are like our father. He thinks deeply and wants to know the reasons behind everything. Not because he is interested in people like you are, but because he understands that with knowledge he increases his power. He's able to make wise decisions for our people." Nantaquaus seemed to concentrate on the rhythm of rowing for a while. "To be chief requires wisdom, but it also requires a willingness to make life-and-death decisions without trying to see all sides like you do."

Pocahontas didn't say anything. She thought her brother would make a wise *Mamanatowic*, but they both knew that when her father died, it would most likely be her uncle, Opechancanough, who took over. He had none of the wisdom and patience of her father. And he hated the *tassantassuk*. She feared he would be a brutal leader.

As they paddled out onto the Chesapeake, Nantaquaus spoke. "Many of the men who reported to our father left some details out of their official report. When they ate with our warriors they told a different tale."

"What did they leave out?" Here Pocahontas thought she had listened in to everything.

"They have tested the *tassantassuk* in a number of different ways. Remember the Arrohattoc who came to see our father?"

"Yes. He was the one who told of Parahunt meeting them."

"What he didn't tell was that, while that group of *tassantassuk* was visiting the villages along the river, more than a hundred warriors attacked the *tassantassuk* village."

Pocahontas drew in a noisy breath. "How many survived?"

"It appears that several were wounded, maybe ten, maybe more. One boy was killed as he tried to find shelter in one of the white bird ships."

"A boy?" Why did Pocahontas feel such a loss? These people were strangers.

"It would have been worse but for the massive thunder-stick hidden on one of their boats that sent a hard, round stone flying into the air with great force. The thunder that boomed shook the chest of every warrior there. The stone—Nauiraus said it is called a cannonshot—hit a tree and broke the tree in half and sent it down onto the warriors."

Pocahontas repeated the word, "Cannonshot. Cannonshot." Now she had one more English word.

"The warriors scattered like a group of scared girls."

Pocahontas kicked her brother in the back. "Stop mocking girls."

"It's just a saying." He laughed. "Of course sayings usually come from wise observations."

She scooped up a handful of water and splashed her brother. She enjoyed seeing the shiver caused by cold water on hot skin.

He put his hands up in a gesture of surrender.

"Why would Nauiraus act as their guide and pretend to be their friend, knowing his people planned an attack?" Pocahontas asked.

"I'm not sure Nauiraus isn't a friend to them. No one can control what the *weroances* do except our father."

"I wish our father would—" Pocahontas stopped mid-sentence. Feeling the stiffened back of her brother ahead of her, she knew he saw it at the same moment. The largest of the white bird boats sailed toward the Great Water.

Nantaquaus began rowing harder on one side of his canoe to guide it toward the mouth of the Powhatan River. Neither spoke until they were well up the river.

"They are leaving," Pocahontas said. Why did she feel

such sorrow at their leaving? "I never got to ask my questions." She knew that wasn't it, though.

"We don't know that they leave. That is only one ship. Remember? We saw three. Soon we will come ashore and hide my canoe. We will come around from behind where the tall grass will shield us."

They hid the canoe in a thick clump of bushes quite a distance from the settlement. They circled around until they could approach the meadow of tall grass from the back. Both brother and sister knew how to move through any terrain without being seen and without making a sound.

They heard the noise of the *tassantassuk* first. Many voices talking.

"They have not all left," Pocahontas said, and she grasped Nantaquaus's arm. She could not say why it meant so much to her that they stayed.

He put his hand over his mouth to signal her to keep her voice down. He needn't have worried. The *tassantassuk* made so much noise—talking, clanging, rasping, singing—they could not have heard an army approaching.

He pointed to an opening in the log wall, where they could see inside. Men were stacking planks of wood. Others were lifting stacks and moving through a gate. Pocahontas and Nantaquaus moved through the grass so they could look toward the river on the opposite side of the encampment. Men were loading the wood onto one of the two ships.

"It looks like that ship is being readied to follow the first out onto the great water," Nantaquaus said. "Maybe they were just visiting for a short time."

Pocahontas studied the parts of the village she could see

through the openings in the wall. "I don't think so." She kept craning her head and silently moving. "No. I see corn planted inside."

Nantaquaus squinted, angling for a better look. "And you call that corn?" The field was sparse at best and the edges of the leaves were brown. "I think the soil here in this marshy ground may have too much salt to allow much to grow. The Paspahegh said this ground is only fit for hunting."

"But the *tassantassuk* would not go to the work of planting just to leave."

"No. You may be right, but that corn will never feed them," Nantaquaus said. "The other problem is the lack of water. Nauiraus said there are no springs on this piece of land. For now they pull water out of the river, but already the water turns slimy and brackish and it is only *nepinough*. What will happen toward the end of summer?"

Pocahontas agreed with her brother. How would they survive? Even though the full heat had not yet come to the land, the swampy ground caused an uncomfortable heat—the water-laden kind you felt when a pot of water was put over the fire. And the biting, blood-sucking insects flew in clouds across the meadow. Had she not been worried about making noise, she would have been swatting insects all day long.

The parade of men carrying wood to the ship continued from the time Pocahontas and Nantaquaus arrived until the sun shone overhead. Many of the men just stood around, pointing and talking. They wore so much clothing. The only pieces of skin that showed were their hands and the parts of their faces not covered with hair—pale skin, not like

Pocahontas's skin. It reminded her of Micah, the boy who came with the Chesapeake captives.

The men who worked wore that hard clothing that caused the sun to glint off of it like sun sometimes does on water. Pocahontas had to shield her eyes sometimes when one of them turned the wrong way. It hurt like looking into the full sun.

"Why are there more men who stand and talk than men who work?" she asked.

"They act like they are chiefs, but why would one tribe have so many chiefs?" Nantaquaus had as many questions as Pocahontas.

"See the little one with dark hair? The one who works the hardest and seems the strongest?" Pocahontas pointed toward the man who had carried the most loads of wood to the ship. "He seems like the real *weroance*, even though those other men strut like they are leaders."

"You may be right. Watch how his eyes keep scanning as he moves. He may be the only real warrior we've seen today. He looks for trouble even when it seems safe. He keeps looking out here, like he is the only one who sees the danger in weeds tall enough to hide a man."

"And he carries his weapon by his side." Pocahontas wanted to remember this *tassantassuk*. She hoped he would come to Werowocomoco to meet with her father. She hoped those idle men would not be the ones to come.

They crouched there in the grass for what seemed like a long time, but Pocahontas could not drag herself away. She kept catching snippets of words she knew. England. Ship. Sail. Cannon. Gold.

When the wood had all been loaded, the line of men began pushing and pulling something heavy from the ship to the village. It looked like a log on its side, but with wheels. She caught the word again—cannon. So that was the weapon that fired a stone big enough to scare off a hundred warriors.

After they managed to push it into the wall, no one came out for a time. Pocahontas waited, but this time without fearing that the people were all leaving. The cannon meant that at least some would stay. The *tassantassuk* never left their weapons. Everyone knew that. She smiled to herself, hoping the little warrior would stay.

When the sun began to cast shadows, the gate opened once more and the whole village seemed to pour out through the opening and move toward the ship. Only her man seemed watchful. The rest talked and laughed, slapping hands on each other's backs.

"They take leave of one another," Nantaquaus whispered.

He was right. Almost half the men climbed aboard the larger of the two ships left in the channel. The others stood and watched. A few boys waved. With loud flaps the great white bird opened her wings and began to move from the shore to open water.

The sight of it took Pocahontas's breath away. "I want to sail on a white bird before I die," she whispered.

Nantaquaus looked at her as if he knew not who spoke those words. "Don't say words like that, sister. The gods cannot like it."

She didn't answer, but deep in her spirit she felt sure *Gitchee Manitou* was the one who planted the longing.

6

Death to the Captive

Pocahontas had managed to talk her brother into spying on the *tassantassuk* several more times. She felt like she was getting to know them. The short warrior she'd noticed on the first visit was her favorite. They called him John Smith. She'd said that name over and over, practicing how it sounded. She now thought of him as John Smith. He worked the hardest and seemed to be the smartest. She often watched him scanning the meadow carefully for movement. She stayed as still as possible, but she suspected he knew she was there.

None of the others seemed aware, including the new *weroance*. They called his name Rat-cliff. The first *weroance* now lived on the small white bird boat and no longer ruled his people. Nantaquaus said they treated him like a captive, so he must have done something wrong.

Each time she and her brother came to the meadow, they could see the changes in the *tassantassuk*. Harvest was finished and it should have been a time of feasting like it was at

Werowocomoco, but these people were starving. She knew the look. And their numbers grew smaller and smaller. She never saw funeral pyres, but she began to realize that the holes they dug in the ground were for their dead. She and Nantaquaus once saw them put a body into the ground. At first they dug holes outside the walls, but more recently she could see through some of the gaps in the wall that they started making the dead holes inside.

"They don't want us to know how many of their warriors have died from sickness," Nantaquaus said one day. Pocahontas knew he guessed right. She could tell by comparing the comings and goings of her first visits with the more recent ones that only a fraction of the *tassantassuk* survived.

It made her sad. Would they all die before she could know them? She had so many questions. Would John Smith die? She hoped not. Each time she came, she held her breath until she saw him. He grew thin but he still worked hard.

"Pocahontas, come look at the storehouse," Nokomias said. The last tribute had been brought and her father and his advisors had assembled in the lodge next to his ceremonial lodge to look over the stores. The storehouse was almost as big as the ceremonial lodge.

She hadn't planned to go because they'd only be talking about the harvest. She never missed listening in on a meeting to discuss the *tassantassuk*, but she didn't care so much about the everyday running of the village.

"I've never seen so much food," Nokomias said.

Pocahontas looked at her friend. Seeing the stores of food must have made Nokomias feel secure. "I'll go with you."

They slipped inside as the men were talking.

"We must be careful with food until the rains come back to the earth," Rawhunt said. He was the oldest.

Nokomias tilted her head to the side as she looked at the stores. "Isn't this enough?" she whispered to Pocahontas.

"It's not as much as in the years when the rains came. We have to have enough to feed all our people until the next harvest—not just Werowocomoco, but other villages if they fall short of food."

Nokomias clasped her hands together and listened to the men.

"Don't look so worried," Pocahontas whispered. "Our father will see that you always have enough food to eat. He just wants us to be careful not to waste."

Two warriors came running into the lodge, brushing by the girls. Powhatan turned. "Do you have news?"

"Yes," the taller man said, bowing his head. "The brother of the great Powhatan captured the *weroance* of the English, the man they call John Smith."

John Smith! Pocahontas drew closer. He was not a *weroance*. She knew that from watching their village. The man called Rat-cliff acted as the English *weroance*.

"Come," her father said, motioning toward his lodge. "Make food for our friends," he said to some of the nearby women. The messengers, her father, and his advisors made their way to the lodge. Pocahontas followed.

"I cannot come," Nokomias said.

"Stay with me. Be silent and you can sneak in."

Nokomias's eyes grew large. "No. I must not. I'll go find Matachanna."

Pocahontas watched her friend leave. She probably should have followed Nokomias, but she couldn't bear to miss the report. She sat down on the edge of the dais as everyone settled into place. Nantaquaus came and sat in the gallery nearest Pocahontas.

"So tell us your news," her father told the messenger, settling in for a full report.

"The one named John Smith sailed with a small band of men in their canoe up the Chickhominy. When they came upon the fast-moving *suckhanna*, they turned their canoe around and sailed back to Apokant, to our village."

Powhatan turned to Parahunt and nodded. "The water is too swift for their kind of canoe. They could not do it without one of our canoes."

"Yes," the Chickhominy envoy said. "That's why they came to us. The man called John Smith—the *weroance*—asked us to give him the use of a canoe and two guides. He said he wanted to hunt upriver."

"You didn't believe him?" Powhatan asked.

"Why would anyone travel so far when geese can still be found everywhere this time of the year?"

"That is what I wondered." Powhatan rubbed his face. "Continue."

"We gave him one of our canoes—a swift one. Our *weroance* sent me and another warrior to go with him. John Smith took two of his men and told the other men to stay behind. They did not join our people in the village. Before he left, John Smith ordered them to stay on their canoe, but our

weroance wanted to discover more about the *tassantassuk*."
The man lowered his head and backed off, gesturing with his
hand to another man from Apokant. "He will tell you what
took place after we left."

Pocahontas could see the second man's hesitation.

"Our *weroance* told the women of the village to lure the
tassantassuk to shore." He glanced at Pocahontas as if to acknowledge that he would choose his words carefully. "They
offered baskets of food and other enticements."

She knew what was coming. Treachery. Why did her
people have to test strangers to see how brave they were? She
wished she could cover her ears or slip out of the lodge so she
wouldn't have to hear the rest. But if she left, she'd miss hearing about John Smith.

"When the *tassantassuk* understood what we planned, six
of them escaped. We had but one to test. They called him
Kay-son. He accounted himself well. He remained coura-
geous to the end."

"So the *tassantassuk* are not cowards?" Powhatan did not
need to ask what kind of trial Kay-son endured. They all
knew.

"The six who escaped never tried to save their brother, so
we do not know about them, but, yes, Kay-son is not a cow-
ard. He died a true warrior."

The other man came forward again. When Powhatan ac-
knowledged him, he said, "I will tell you about John Smith.
After we went upstream, John Smith asked us to join him to
hunt. His two men stayed with the canoe."

Pocahontas had watched John Smith many times. She
knew his boldness, but going off alone—did he not know to

keep his warriors close? She looked at her brother to see if he was surprised. He did not seem surprised by any of this. Instead, he looked at her and nodded his head.

Nantaquaus knew.

She thought about it. Of course, he knew. He knew everything that had happened. He'd been hunting with their uncle's people. The moment Nantaquaus stood up to leave the ceremonial lodge, she'd be on his heels. He could probably tell her the whole story.

The envoy continued speaking. "We did not expect a war party, but we heard a scream from one of John Smith's men. Then silence. We knew someone had attacked."

"Did you know who?" Powhatan asked.

"Not then. We had stepped out of the canoe into the water. Before we could wade to shore, we heard the calls of a war party. An arrow hit John Smith here." He pointed to his thigh.

Pocahontas inhaled deeply. That place carried a deep stream of blood. Many warriors died from having that life-giving stream pierced. She longed to ask if John Smith lived, but after one look at her father's stern face she kept quiet.

"Your brother Opechancanough led the warriors. I called out and warned him that John Smith was a *weroance*. I told him the man must not be killed. I knew he must be brought to you. During the whoops and thrashing about we stepped backward toward the shore. Both John Smith and I stepped into the sucking sand."

That quicksand had swallowed many an unsuspecting person.

"The warriors pulled us to safety. As they pulled John Smith onto the bank, Opechancanough's men raised their clubs."

Powhatan leaned forward. Pocahontas knew that if her uncle had killed John Smith, a man whom they believed to be a chief, it would have been an open challenge to the great Powhatan. A *weroance* of any kind was a valuable captive.

"John Smith raised something of his own above his head. It caught the sun like *mattassin*. Your brother Opechancanough put his hand up to stop the warriors while John Smith showed this—this com-pass he had." His voice lowered. "It is strong medicine. It could guide a warrior in a strange place. Even when John Smith moved, the com-pass pointed toward the direction of the star-that-guides."

"Did you bring me that com-pass?" Powhatan asked, holding out his hand.

"No. Opechancanough will bring it when he brings John Smith."

Now it was Pocahontas's turn to lean forward. John Smith? Coming here to Werowocomoco?

She could concentrate on little else. The envoy told her father that John Smith had been taken to Rasawrack, her uncle's hunting camp, but she hardly heard him. She caught her brother's eye and silently begged him to leave. She had to hear the rest of the story.

When the women brought more food, Nantaquaus left with Pocahontas following. They crossed the culvert into the village, but before they even reached the downed log, Pocahontas began asking questions.

"Did you see him? Why didn't you tell me? Is he hurt?"

"Slow down and give me a chance to answer." Nantaquaus laughed. "I didn't tell you because I just returned from Rasawrack."

"Is that where our uncle took John Smith?"

"Yes. They first arrived about the time I arrived. No one wanted to hunt after that."

"Did they test him?" Pocahontas pressed her lips together.

"Not by torture. The men did a war dance. That should have been enough to scare most *tassantassuk*, but John Smith only seemed interested. He admired the paint on the faces of the warriors and tried to mimic the war cries and the sound of the women's screams."

Pocahontas laughed. She couldn't even do the wavery, high-pitched ululations that the women did with the muscles of their throats. It sounded almost like a coyote howling. She'd like to see a man try.

"As he watched, John Smith kept scratching a goose feather on . . . something he called paper."

"Paper?" Pocahontas tried the word out.

"I couldn't stop watching. It seemed like some kind of magic." Nantaquaus seemed to consider it. "He did not draw pictures. He put marks. Something like the marks a bird makes when he walks on wet sand. When he finished marking the paper, he folded it and asked our uncle to have it taken to his people. He said the paper would tell his people what he wanted them to send back as gifts to our uncle."

"Did Opechancanough send it?"

"He did, but he also wanted to test if it was magic or some kind of trick."

Pocahontas had wondered the same thing.

"Our uncle instructed his men to stay silent as they gave the paper to the *tassantassuk*. Not to give any hints or even cast their eyes toward any of the things John Smith asked his people to send. Even though the men said nothing, John Smith's men looked at the paper and gathered together the very things John Smith requested of them."

Pocahontas thought about it. "It's not magic. He's not a medicine man."

"We've observed him. He's a warrior."

"So do you think he has found a way of putting his words on that paper? A way that lets other people somehow get the words off that paper?"

"I do."

Pocahontas didn't speak right away. "I want to learn to put my words on a paper," she whispered. "And I want to know how to understand other people's words on paper."

Nantaquaus smiled. "The only words on your paper would be questions."

Pocahontas ignored him. "Is John Smith badly injured?"

"No, the arrow did not go deep. You'll see for yourself. Our uncle should be arriving with him by sundown."

"I'm going to be there," Pocahontas said.

She went to her lodge and gathered her things to bathe. Matachanna and Nokomias caught up and went with her down to the river. It was too cold to get into the water, but they took a clay pot to scoop out water to wash their faces and hands. The girls had to break a thin layer of ice on the water. The snows had not yet come, but the few stragglers of geese flying overhead reminded Pocahontas that *popanow*—winter —had settled on the land.

Though she loved the long warm days of summer, these short, dark days held a mysterious beauty. The rabbits already wore white coats. Soon she'd see their soft footprints in the snow. The once-noisy forest stood silent since most of the animals stayed warm, hidden deep in their dens. The trees were bare and the ice crunched on the ground first thing in the morning.

As she dressed she put on layers of soft hide and thick fur. Although she could no longer walk on her hands with so much clothing, the mothers told her she looked prettiest in the cold weather with her face framed in the long fur mantle of the fox. She looked into the clear stream. Yes, the cold had tinted her cheeks the color of berries. She opened the pouch with her necklaces and put them all on, touching the one with Anna's water bead.

"This is my favorite necklace, Nokomias," she said, touching her friend's arm.

"You like it because of the English bead, don't you?" Matachanna asked.

"Partly." Something deep inside her was drawn to the English. She didn't know why, but she couldn't stop thinking about them. "I want to know all about them." She rubbed her hands against the cold. "But mostly I love the necklace because you gave us our beads when you shared your story with us."

Nokomias smiled. "That was when I stopped being a captive and became a sister."

They heard dogs barking and children excitedly squealing —the kind of disturbance that marked the arrival of visitors in the village.

"Here come the Pamunkeys, Opechancanough, and the captive," Matachanna said. "Are you going to go, Pocahontas?"

"I am."

Nokomias hung back. "You go. I need to go to Alaqua."

"I'm sure Alaqua will be there in the village with every-one else." Pocahontas knew that seeing a party arrive with captives would bring back memories for her friend. "Come with me and we'll find Alaqua."

"I'll stay with you, Nokomias." Matachanna linked arms with her.

Pocahontas helped them find Alaqua, who was preparing *ponepone* and roasting a goose for a feast. She left the two girls there to help.

By the time she got to the Great Lodge, a crowd had al-ready gathered. She couldn't make her way to her usual place on the dais without pushing through nearly half the people of her village and more visiting dignitaries than Pocahontas had ever seen gathered at Werowocomoco. Of course, from where she stood she could barely see at all. And with the noise—whoops and jeers—she couldn't hear much either.

Everyone had prepared for this. The warriors and many of the women had streaked their faces with earth, ash, and pocone red. The colors and designs added to the excitement. Jewelry flashed in the firelight. As the crowd jostled and parted a little, she saw her father. He wore ropes of pearls along with his other necklaces.

As she pushed forward a little, she saw the large sullen woman, one of the wives of the Appomattoc *weroance*, bring water for John Smith to wash his hands. Then the woman slowly lifted her hand, looking around to make sure everyone was aware of her elevated status, and signaled for some of the mothers to come in with food. Pocahontas smelled the rich corn *ponepone* that must have just came out of Alaqua's clay oven. The women came in with baskets of food—venison, goose, sturgeon, *ponepone*, walnuts, and berries.

"That may be his last meal." Nantaquaus had come and stood beside her. "There is much to distrust in the English."

Pocahontas knew that her brother was right. This may very well be John Smith's last meal. With her father, one never knew. She only knew that if it looked like he was to be tested or killed, she would leave. She couldn't bear to see it.

As the captive ate, her father asked him questions. Pocahontas was surprised by how far John Smith's grasp of language had come. When she first began spying on him, he could speak almost no Powhatan. She used to cover her mouth to keep from laughing when she watched him try to converse with one of the warriors outside the English village.

"Why have your people come to our land?" Powhatan stopped eating, leaned back, and folded his arms across his chest.

John Smith told a story of a fight with the *Espaniuks*—he called them Spanish—and a ship that needed repair. He chose his words carefully and pronounced them slowly. He said the English only waited for the bigger ships to come take them away.

"That doesn't sound true." Nantaquaus narrowed his eyes. "If that were so, why are they building and exploring?"

"Now who's asking questions?" Pocahontas poked him. "I wonder if your wise English friend is saying what he thinks our father and his advisors want to hear?"

"Maybe, but our father is not easily fooled." Nantaquaus shifted. "Look at the great Powhatan's face though. He admires John Smith. I can see it in his eyes."

"I can't see his face. I can't see anything but a whole lodge of backsides."

Nantaquaus put his hand over his mouth to keep from laughing. "Come, let's try to push our way further. When people see that it is the princess trying to push her way through, those people should move for you."

Pocahontas followed the path made by her brother as they inched their way toward their usual places.

When John Smith finished eating, one of the mothers came forward and held a bowl of water toward him for washing and a bunch of feathers for drying. Her father had finished his questioning.

A group of warriors stood near the dais with their war clubs. The whole time John Smith had been answering questions they had rhythmically hit their hands with the heads of the clubs, as if they were itching to connect those clubs to flesh.

"Look," Nantaquaus said.

Powhatan lifted his arms and a group of warriors brought in two large flat stones and laid them below the dais.

Pocahontas could feel the blood pound in her head. She inched closer, even though she knew she should be moving toward the door. She didn't want to see what she guessed would come next, but for some reason, she couldn't abandon the scene.

John Smith was brought forward and lowered to the stones. The men with war clubs gathered around. Drums began to beat. Women started dancing and making their throaty sounds.

Pocahontas felt lightheaded. Her breath came out as if

she'd been running—short, fast breaths. She found herself whispering, "No, no, no," to the beat of the drum.

The noise in the room got louder but she felt as if she were underwater. Time slowed down. The noise became muffled and she somehow felt a Presence—the presence of *Gitchee Manitou*. Even the beat of her heart slowed and she raised her head, breathing air slowly into her lungs. She remembered the night when she felt the Great Spirit say, "*Amosens*, I have given you a heart to know Me. Search your heart."

And now, she felt Him again. In the middle of the chaos of her father's lodge, she knew the Spirit was present. As the crowd surrounding the captive came back into focus, she watched the warriors raise their clubs high above the head of John Smith.

"No!" she shouted, as she pushed forward and threw her body over John Smith, cradling his head in her arms.

She tensed, waiting for that first fatal blow of a war club to fall on her.

7
Living at Peace

The blow never came. Pocahontas could feel her brother's hands lift her off the captive and stand her up, facing her father. The dancing had ceased. No one spoke.

"*Amosens*, come." Her father motioned for her to come closer.

She could see open hostility on the faces of many of her father's advisors. What had made her throw herself over a *tassantassa* about to be clubbed to death? As she asked that question, she knew the answer.

She walked toward her father. This would be one time she could not count on laughter, somersaults, and teasing to ease the tension.

"Can you tell me what my daughter intended by that spectacle?" Her father kept his hands clasped in his lap.

"I could not bear the thought of John Smith being killed."

"And what do you know of this John Smith?"

"I have watched him at his village. He cares for his people, he cares for the land, and he seeks to understand us and honor us."

"You've seen all that?"

"And I saw how brave he was today."

"Do you think I gave the order to kill him?" her father asked.

Pocahontas started to answer yes, but stopped. Could this have been some kind of ceremony? She knew the Powhatan people had a rite of adoption into the tribe. She'd never seen it, but she'd heard it involved an enactment of death to life. Could that be what had been happening? Had she made a fool of herself for nothing?

"You ask many questions in your mind, do you not?" Powhatan's mouth twitched. "Now you will never know if the captive would have been killed or spared."

"I am sorry, Father."

"Do not be sorry, little one. You proved your own bravery. There is no greater sacrifice than to lay down your life for another."

Even the advisors murmured their approval. Opechancanough glared, but the other faces on the dais relaxed.

"So, you have saved the captive, John Smith." Her father smiled at her. "What do you propose we do with him now?"

Pocahontas remained silent for a minute. She hadn't considered that. "He could stay in our village to help us learn about his people."

"Perhaps."

"He can teach us English and I can teach him our language."

Her father nodded, as if waiting for more.

"He can make hatchets for you and bells, beads, and *mattassin* jewelry for me."

At that the great Powhatan laughed. Pocahontas looked over at the captive and saw that he'd understood enough to make him smile as well.

⚜ ⚜ ⚜ ⚜

"Tell me you did not do what they say you did?" Matachanna caught up with Pocahontas before she reached their sleeping lodge. "Everyone is talking about it. You could have been killed."

Pocahontas slowed down. The reality of what she did had only just begun to sink in.

"And even though you didn't get killed, you had to face our father. That's worse." Matachanna never asked the obvious question—Why?

"I know. I acted on impulse. I didn't have time to think about all that." Pocahontas didn't know how to put into words why she acted. Her people's god, Okeus, never spoke. She couldn't remember one time that someone claimed to have heard from or even had a thought from Okeus. No, Okeus did things to them—gave them sun, withheld rain, caused the sturgeon to thrive, took someone's baby in death. He certainly didn't speak to her people in their spirits. Not even to the medicine man.

No, this Spirit, *Gitchee Manitou*, the Great Spirit, was different from Okeus. She knew it. She wanted to listen for His voice again.

"You are my older sister, the favorite of our great father,

and I am supposed to serve you and respect you. But Pocahontas, you mustn't be so heedless." A catch in Matachanna's
voice gave away the depth of her concern. "I cannot imagine
what I would do without you."

Pocahontas stopped and hugged this little sister. "Nor I
you." She put her playful face back. "So what are the people
saying?"

Matachanna laughed. "You would think about that,
wouldn't you?" They walked a little farther. Once the sun
went down the air grew cold. On a night like tonight with the
wind blowing, it felt colder than when it snowed. "If you
must know, some are beginning to craft stories and songs
about your bravery."

Pocahontas laughed. "And the others?"

"I'm not going to say."

Pocahontas knew what Matachanna didn't want to say.
Some resented her position with her father and hated any in-
terference. Others resisted change of any kind. They saw the
English arrival on their shores as a dangerous threat to the
Powhatan world. They probably would have seen the killing
of John Smith as a useful warning to the *tassantassuk*.

That night, as the girls crawled under their blankets and
furs, Matachanna asked, "So now that you saved him, what
are you going to do with him?"

"He becomes our brother now. I will go to him tomorrow
morning and learn everything I can about him and his people."

Matachanna laughed. "You are going to treat him just like
Nantaquaus, aren't you? You are going to bombard him with
questions until he wishes he had been clubbed to death and
put out of his misery."

Pocahontas woke long before dawn. She lay quietly so as not to wake her sister. She could watch her breath, even inside the lodge, snuggled next to Matachanna. How she wished she could tell if snow were coming like Powhatan could. She listened to the morning sounds. The rustling in the village always started early with the mothers building the fires and making their way to the river for water. She usually smelled corn cooking as she woke. This morning she woke before the mothers.

She slipped out of her covers and put on her furs to walk out toward the marshes where she could find a bit of privacy. How she envied the English their little hut—didn't they call it a privy?

By the time she washed in the icy water and headed back toward the lodge, Matachanna's mother was stirring the pot.

"Will you take food to the captive when it has finished cooking?"

"The captive? You mean John Smith?"

"How many captives do we have in this village, little one?" The mother smiled at her. "I remember. When Nokomias came we had this same talk. You do not like the idea of captives."

"But he's not a captive. He is an ally, now."

"We shall see what your father does before we know what to call the *tassantassa*."

Pocahontas helped put the food in a basket and carried it over to the lodge where they had put John Smith. As she got closer she saw him sitting outside.

"So it is the princess," he said, bowing his head.

She was not familiar with this gesture.

"I owe my life to you." He patted his hand against his heart. She did know what that meant—it meant friend.

She patted her own chest. "Are you well?"

"Yes. I am well."

Pocahontas wished she could really talk to this man she felt she knew. She handed him the food and sat down nearby. "I watched you."

"Last night?" He looked puzzled. "While I slept?"

She smiled for the first time. "No. I watched you at your village. My brother Nantaquaus and I came often to watch your people."

Now it was his turn to smile. "I thought you looked familiar. I think I saw you in the tall grass a time or two." He used the oyster shell to scrape the last bits of corn out of the bowl. "What did you see?"

She got up to take the gourd from him, leaving him the basket of berries. "I saw many strange things. I saw no women. Who does your work? Who plants food? Who gets water? Who cooks?"

"We have no women with us, so we must do all those things."

"Why do you cut trees and slice them into boards and put them on your *quintans*—your ship?"

John Smith seemed to hesitate, rubbing his hand along the hair on his face.

"You may tell me truth," Pocahontas said with a smile, "instead of the stories you told my father about the *Espaniuks* and repairs."

John Smith laughed. "You are nothing if not direct, are you not? And how will I know that you won't carry every story I tell to your father?"

"You ask just as many questions as me." She almost turned a somersault. Had she not been bundled in fur she would have. It always made talking easier when she moved. "Have I told my father all the things I observed at your village? No."

"I want to learn more about your people, and I sense that you want to learn more about my people." He patted the ground beside him, signaling to her to sit down.

She sat, putting her hands one over the other signaling that she waited.

"I will tell you true and you must pledge to tell me true." He also sat silently while he waited for her answer.

"I observed you at your village. I know you are a wise man. You work even when others are idle. When you thought you were to die, you stayed silent; you did not beg for mercy." She looked at him through narrowed eyes. "I pledge."

"Then we are friends." He repeated the word in English.

"Friends." She said the English word slowly and put her hand against her chest.

The captors had not tethered John Smith, so he stood and stretched his legs. "It appears I'm free to move about the village. Will you go with me for a walk?"

"Yes. I told my father, the great Powhatan, I would learn about your people and you will learn about my people. We'll walk." She scooped up the gourd and basket and they took those to the cooking pit outside her sleeping lodge.

As she showed him some of her favorite places in the village, a group of boys and dogs began to follow. One boy reached out to touch John Smith's sleeve. He stopped and the boy bolted.

Pocahontas called out, "*Maraowanchesso!*" The boy reluctantly came back.

"What does that word mean?" John Smith asked.

Pocahontas pointed to the boy.

"Is that his name?"

"No." She pointed to each boy, repeating the word.

"Oh." He drew the sound of the word out, nodding his head. "It means *boy*. They are all boys."

"Boy," she repeated, clapping her hands.

Each boy repeated the word as well. She could hear a chorus of "boy." She knew they'd be hearing that word in the village until they grew sick of it.

John Smith stooped down to let the boy feel the cloth of his shirt. Pocahontas felt it as well. It wasn't like skin. When she looked closer she could see that it was made of the finest threads she'd ever seen. Her people used fibers for embroidery, but these fibers were like nothing they had. She smelled it. It didn't smell as if it came from animals.

"It's a trifle dirty from the scuffle in the river."

Pocahontas could tell that she embarrassed him by smelling it. "I smell not for cleanliness but to see what manner of animal."

"It's not from an animal, it is good solid English linen."

"Linen."

The boys ran off with dogs following them. Pocahontas knew they had hoped for more excitement from this *tassantassa*.

"It comes from a plant—from flax." He paused. "How much English do you know?"

"Ship. Sailing ship. England, pirates. King. Cannonshot. Friend—"

"You have certainly learned a number of words." He smiled. "Do you have any others?"

She nodded. "Rat-cliff."

John Smith frowned. "I like you putting the emphasis on rat."

"Compass. Gold—"

"Gold?" He stood up again. "Tell me what you know about gold. Where did you hear that word?"

"You ask as many questions as I do." Pocahontas laughed. She wondered what Nantaquaus would think of John Smith's questions. Maybe it wasn't just girls who asked questions.

"Princess, tell me about gold." John Smith started walking, lengthening his strides. Pocahontas had to skip to keep up with him.

"Gold, gold, gold. When I watched your village, I heard that word more often than any other word."

They got to the edge of the river and John Smith pointed to the downed tree trunk. "Please, sit down." He waited for her to sit and then he seated himself a distance from her. The water ran so clear, they could see shapes of fish moving silently through the water.

"What does that word mean?"

John Smith held out his hand and pointed to a ring on his finger. "This is made of gold. It is like *mattassin*—copper—only softer."

"I thought the word meant this." Pocahontas reached down and scooped up a handful of dirt.

"Dirt? Why would you think that?"

"Because your men dig and dig in the dirt, the whole time talking about gold."

"Gold comes from the ground. They dig to find it."

"We do not have anything like that in our ground." She touched his ring. "No, nothing like gold."

"I have begun to suspect that," John Smith said, almost as if speaking to himself. "If you had gold, why would you not have necklaces made of it, like those people the Spanish encountered on their expeditions?"

Pocahontas didn't understand many of his words even though most of them were in her language.

John Smith turned to look at her. "We said we would speak the truth to each other. You asked about the planks of lumber—the slices of trees you saw us loading onto the ships."

"Lumber," she repeated.

"The people who sent us from England are businessmen. They are in the business of trade."

Pocahontas understood trade. "You mean like exchanging tools for food?"

"Yes. They sent us here to explore this new land—"

Pocahontas laughed. "Our land is not new. It has been our home for as many moons as our stories recall."

Now John Smith laughed. "Yes, it's different seeing it through your eyes." He reached over and ran his hand in the cold water. "What I meant to say is that our people sent us to find gold and send back lumber. They want treasure in exchange for giving us food and supplies for this expedition."

"I don't think they gave you enough food," Pocahontas said quietly. She didn't mean to criticize, but anyone with eyes could see that their village starved.

"This is true," he said. "And I think we did indeed find treasure, but it's not to be the gold they seek."

"So what is the treasure?"

"Look around you. Your land is the most beautiful land I've ever seen—rich with possibilities and—"

Nantaquaus interrupted his words as he came running toward them. "John Smith, my father, the great Powhatan, wishes to speak to you."

Pocahontas felt her friend stiffen. *He may trust me, but he still does not trust my father.* She loved and respected her father, but John Smith had reason to fear. Who could ever know what her father would do?

8

Royal Visit to Jamestown

Pocahontas and Nantaquaus walked with John Smith. As they came to the ceremonial lodge, Pocahontas wondered what kind of thoughts went through her friend's mind. Only yesterday, they all believed this would be the place of his death.

Her father sat at his customary place. Pocahontas could tell that he respected John Smith. He wore his finest clothing and all of his necklaces and earrings. His advisors wore their finery as well.

"Come, John Smith. Sit." He pointed to the gallery nearest his throne. "I wish to speak to you."

John Smith sat down. Nantaquaus sat next to him while Pocahontas took her favorite spot near her father.

"My daughter saved your life last night." He said it in his plain way of speaking. "Do you know what that makes you?"

John Smith did not answer. He leaned forward.

"That makes you her brother. You have become my adopted son."

Pocahontas smiled. This was good. No one would harm John Smith if her father claimed him as a member of the tribe.

"You shall be at home here in Werowocomoco. You may go anywhere you want to go."

"Thank you, great Powhatan. I am honored to be your son."

Powhatan nodded his head.

"I am honored by your invitation to remain here, but I must go back to my own village. Captain Newport may be coming back with his ships any day, with news from our king."

"What is this king?"

"He is the *Mamanatowic* of the English people. Just as you are the king of your people." John Smith put out his hand palm up toward Powhatan. "Just as you sit on your throne and rule your people, our king rules our people."

"And who is this Captain Newport? Is he another *weroance* of your people?"

Pocahontas watched her friend. She knew he was not a *weroance*, but she also knew that it was important he seem so to her father. She wondered if John Smith knew this.

"Captain Newport is like . . . he's like my father."

Pocahontas smiled. That kind of ceremonial connection could easily be understood.

"Your father . . ." Powhatan turned to some of his advisors and they carried on a whispered conversation. "We know you want to travel back to your village. Opechancanough has your boat—the one you call a shallop."

Pocahontas's uncle didn't look too happy about having to return the shallop.

"We know you will want to give your new family gifts."

John Smith smiled in agreement.

"We wish for a grinding stone and two of your firesticks."

Pocahontas saw the color drain out of John Smith's face, but he did not let on there was any trouble. She had watched the English long enough to know that the one thing they wouldn't part with was their weapons. She understood their reticence. If her father had those firesticks, the world would no longer be a safe place for the Iroquois and maybe not for the English either.

"I will do it," John Smith said.

Pocahontas looked from his face to her brother's face. She saw the same surprise on her brother's face that she felt.

"But rather than give you these small broken firesticks, if your men follow me to my village I will give them our greatest guns to carry home along with our best grinding stone."

Her father's advisors looked stunned at first, and then wide smiles broke out on their faces. Pocahontas could tell that each one was picturing himself with an English gun. Her father wore that bemused expression that told her he knew things were not as they seemed. There was nothing the great Powhatan liked better than a contest of wills. She figured he understood that John Smith had not really given in quite so easily.

As they filed out of the lodge, her father appointed the men who would travel with John Smith. He looked at her and smiled. "You may go in Nantaquaus's canoe and watch John Smith offer his gifts to me."

"Doesn't it feel strange to be traveling to the English village out in the open?" Pocahontas had been so used to watching for her brother, making sure they wouldn't be seen by the *tassantassuk*. Now here they were following the English shallop into the harbor by the place they called Jamestown.

"I wish I knew why our father wanted us to observe the exchange of gifts. When he sent us, I sensed he had a definite reason for us to go."

As the shallop was tied up by the inlet, many of the English came down to the water's edge to greet John Smith.

"We have gifts to exchange with our friends," he called out.

The men sent by her father to bring back the gifts climbed out of the shallop and stood near John Smith.

"Gifts?" One Englishman ran back to what they called the fort and came back with a basket filled with copper and beads.

"No," John Smith said. "They wish for guns and a grinding stone. I promised them our largest."

Pocahontas could see from their faces that they thought him crazy. The man called Rat-cliff stood with his legs apart and his hands on his hips.

"Bring the demiculverins," John Smith shouted. "I promised our finest weaponry for the great Powhatan." A group of Englishmen went into the fort. After a time the gate opened and they came into view, straining to pull great ropes attached to two gigantic cannons.

Once they managed to get the cannons outside of the fort,

John Smith said, "Show them how they fire." He pointed to a tree encrusted with icicles—a beautiful natural ice sculpture. A man fired one of the cannons, jumping out of the way as it lurched backward.

Pocahontas could feel the percussion in her chest. Her ears hurt with the sound. The stones that flew from the belly of the gun severed three tree limbs. The noise of the explosion and the sound of the crashing icicles sent her father's men running for cover.

John Smith laughed. "Come," he said. "Get your guns and your grindstone."

Pocahontas looked at her brother. She could see that he did not laugh. "Our people could never move those guns or that grindstone, could they?"

"No. And your friend knew that." Nantaquaus's voice wore a cold, angry tone that she rarely heard from her brother.

"I think our father knew that as well." Pocahontas thought for a minute. "Yes, he was expecting something like this. I saw it in his face."

Nantaquaus didn't say anything at first, but eventually he nodded his head. "I believe you are right, little sister. In fact, I think our father will laugh when he hears this story."

John Smith had his people bring out baskets of beads, some tools, and beautiful pieces of copper. "Since your men are unable to carry the guns and the grindstone in their canoe, Nantaquaus, please take these gifts to your father as a token of my esteem."

Nantaquaus took the gifts without saying anything. He wrapped them in a hide and tucked the package into his canoe.

"And, Princess, there are no words I can use to thank you

for the gift of life. When you next return to Jamestown, I will have some gifts for you."

The next return. Pocahontas could hardly wait.

᭐

Pocahontas heard someone calling her name outside her sleeping lodge. Nantaquaus. She threw off the furs and blankets and stepped outside. "The sun is still sleeping. What are you doing, waking me?"

He pointed toward the river. The glow from the rising sun lit the sky. "Our father wants us to go to the *tassantassuk* village. We shall take food along as a gift."

Pocahontas remembered the gifts John Smith promised her. "Let me go down to the river to wash before I dress."

"You may bring Nokomias and Matachanna if you like."

Pocahontas thought about that. Part of her wanted to go alone with Nantaquaus. She liked that she had a special kinship with John Smith, but she knew the girls would love the adventure. Besides, the trip itself would be so much more fun if they all went.

"You wake Matachanna and I'll ask Alaqua if Nokomias can go." He started off but turned to shout, "Meet us at my canoe."

When all was ready to go, they pushed off, headed downriver.

"This reminds me of that trip when your canoe was new." Nokomias couldn't hide the excitement in her voice.

"And we saw the sailing ships for the first time." Matachanna sat directly behind Nantaquaus this time. Nokomias sat behind her and Pocahontas sat in the very back. "It was much warmer then," she said, pulling the fur robe around her.

Snow had fallen for two days and, though the sun shone today, she shivered with each gust of wind. The edges of the river were frozen with a covering of snow, making the river seem narrower. The canoe sliced through the water in silence. All sound seemed muffled by the snow. With the advent of winter, no birds chattered, the geese had flown away, and even the deer were rarely seen.

Pocahontas spoke in a whisper. "Doesn't it seem as if we are the only creatures moving through the land?" She pulled her fur mantle closer to her face.

"Are you afraid to go to the *tassantassuk* village?" Nokomias asked.

"No. John Smith is our brother. He will not let harm befall us," Pocahontas said.

Nantaquaus continued to pull the oars through the water. "Do you not think I can protect you, little Nokomias?"

Matachanna laughed. "You can protect three girls against a whole village? I think I'll count on our English brother's friendship."

"That is the difference between a warrior and a girl," Nantaquaus said. "You trust and we remain wary."

"Look." Pocahontas pointed toward the bay. "One of the white bird ships has returned." Moored next to the small ship —the one John Smith called the *Discovery*—was a larger one. "That's not one of the ships we saw before, is it?"

"No. This is a different one. It sits higher in the water." Nantaquaus squinted as if to fix the other ship in his mind. "We've never seen this one."

Pocahontas began to wonder if the story John Smith told to the great Powhatan was true after all. Would he be leaving on this new ship?

As they came to the island, they rowed right to the shore. They no longer had to hide the canoe and crouch among the grasses. Nantaquaus took off his moccasins. With a sharp intake of breath, he stepped into the water, crunching the ice shelf along the edge. He pulled his canoe up on the beach and helped the girls step out onto the sand.

"That's another difference between a warrior and a girl," he said as he dried his feet with a bunch of turkey feathers before putting his moccasins back on.

Pocahontas brushed an imaginary drop of water off her white leather moccasins with great exaggeration. "Some differences are good differences."

Matachanna and Nokomias laughed.

"Their guards have seen us. Here comes a group out to meet us." Nantaquaus reached for his bow, slung over his back.

The group of Englishmen moved cautiously toward them. The three men and a boy all had guns at the ready.

"Hold fire." One of the men put up his hand. "It's the princess. Someone run get Cap'n Smith."

They stood there—Powhatan and English—silently looking at one another, waiting for John Smith.

He came hurrying out through the large gate, after opening it wide. Many other men stood at the opening. "Pocahontas, Nantaquaus, Matachanna, and . . ." he searched for her name as he walked toward them.

"Nokomias," Pocahontas supplied.

"That's right. And Nokomias. Welcome to Jamestown." He reached them and put his hand over his heart. "Welcome."

"We have answered your invitation and come to see your town and meet your people," Pocahontas replied with formality. She felt shy in front of an audience of Englishmen.

"Come," he said. "Come."

He put his hand on Pocahontas's shoulder as they walked toward the group standing just inside the fort. "This is the princess," he said in English. "It is she who saved my life."

He translated this into Powhatan for his guests, but Pocahontas had understood some of what he had spoken in English. She didn't know why that pleased her so much.

"These are two of her maidens and her brother Nantaquaus. Make them welcome."

He motioned to a tall platform on four legs. "Please come sit at my table."

So that was a table. He gestured toward smaller platforms. Pocahontas looked around the village and saw several people seated on these platforms.

"Please. Have a seat on this chair."

Chair. Tables and chairs. Nantaquaus stood back with his arms crossed over his chest, but Nokomias and Matachanna perched themselves on chairs. Matachanna giggled. Pocahontas silently agreed it felt strange.

"Let me get you something to drink," John Smith said as he stood and went inside the square wooden lodge.

He returned with four metal containers and set one in front of each girl. He handed the last to Nantaquaus. Pocahontas put her hands around it. It was shaped like a cylinder of a tree limb, but it was hollow and cold to the touch.

"Cup," he said. "Pewter cup."

Cup. Pewter cup.

He went inside again and came back with something that looked a little like a metal water gourd, only with a handle.

"Pewter?" Pocahontas asked.

"Yes. Pewter pitcher."

Pitcher, pitcher.

He poured a small amount of liquid into each cup. Standing off to the side, Pocahontas noticed one of the young boys watching them. He pressed his lips together and inhaled, while his tongue came out as if to catch an imaginary drop of liquid. *He's hungry. He wishes he had this small bit of liquid for himself.*

She put the cup to her lips and watched the boy's tongue moisten his lips again. *Could this mash be their only food?* The liquid tasted strange to her—like spoiled grain. "Thank you, John Smith, but we are not used to this taste. May we have water instead?"

She looked over at the boy, hoping John Smith would give the cup to him, but instead, her friend took the cups and carefully poured the liquid back into the pitcher, making sure not to spill a drop. He took another pitcher and filled the cups full of cold water.

They all drank deeply.

John Smith saw Nantaquaus looking toward the cannons. "Would you like to go over there and have a good look at them?"

Nantaquaus nodded.

"Perkins," John Smith called to a man standing nearby, "will you take our friend over to the bulwarks and let him have a close-up look at the guns?"

The man came and gestured to Nantaquaus to follow. Matachanna and Nokomias made eye contact with Pocahontas as if to ask if they could get off the chairs and follow.

"Go along with him if you'd like," Pocahontas said.

The girls scooted off their seats and ran to catch up to the men.

"Is it good to be back in your own village?" Pocahontas asked. She noticed that John Smith looked thinner than when he left Werowocomoco.

He smiled. "There is much work to be done."

"We see that the ship came back." She longed to ask hundreds of questions. What made her shy? "Will you all be leaving on the ship?"

"No. This ship came to bring supplies."

"Good. Supplies. So you now have enough food?" She looked over at the dried stalks of what had been their garden inside the walls of their village. She had seen the field during growing season and it looked sparse and stunted then. Now she could tell that the harvest had been pitiful. It couldn't have been more than a week's ration for the men.

"We should have. When the *John and Francis* docked— that's the name of the ship—the first thing they did was unload food. It looked like we were saved starvation." He stopped talking, as if he caught himself.

"Do not fear that I will tell my father that you are in a weakened state. You are my brother. I will not tell." She put her hand on his arm. "You know that all through the growing season we came and watched." She leaned in closer and spoke softly. "From the tall grasses, nearly everything can be seen through breaches in the walls. We observed the troubles—

people not working, men getting sick." She lowered her voice. "We even knew about the men dying. You did not bring the bodies out because you feared to have us know that your numbers dwindled. We saw all that and still we did not tell."

"You are my friend, Pocahontas." John Smith put his hand over his heart again.

"What happened with the supplies brought by this new ship?"

"The ship brought about sixty new colonists and it brought fresh supplies—enough to get us through the winter."

"This is good then?"

"Seven days after it landed, one of the new settlers knocked over a lantern and started a fire. See." He pointed toward the well where men were drawing water. She hadn't noticed before. All that remained of some structures were bits of charred timber. "We lost many of our shelters, but those can be rebuilt." He paused, looking at the devastation. "But we lost the storehouse with all the food."

Pocahontas understood how serious this was. "What will you do? You cannot grow more food in winter."

"I must trade for food."

Pocahontas remained silent.

"Do you think I will have trouble trading for food?"

"I do not know. Little rain has fallen on the land for the last two growing seasons. The grain in our storehouses is low, but we always share what we have. Who can enjoy a full belly if his neighbor starves?"

"So what concerns you?"

"There are so many different villages—different tribes.

Some are friendly. Some are enemies. Some may seem friendly but they are not. How do you know where to go to trade?"

"Are they not all part of your father's empire?"

"They are, but it is an alliance loosely held. They pay homage to my father but he does not tell them who their friends are or who their enemies are. Each tribe has its own *weroance*." She shook her head. "It's hard to explain."

"No. You've explained well." He stood up. "Come. Enough of this serious talk. I don't think I've heard you laugh one single time since you stepped foot in Jamestown. I'm going to start suspecting this is not my princess."

She hopped off the chair.

As he showed her around the village, she saw many things she'd never seen before. She could see how useful many of them would be. Some, like their clothing, were strange. She couldn't imagine anyone wearing all those things, especially in summer when it felt too hot for any amount of clothing.

Her laughter bubbled to the surface when she saw a man rolling a barrel across the grounds. It looked so strange, but she had to admit the shape of the barrel made it easier to move heavy objects.

"Princess, I would like you to meet Captain Newport." John extended his hand to an older man.

"Captain Newport, this is the daughter of the great Powhatan, Pocahontas."

"Good day," she said in English. She turned to John Smith and spoke in her language. "This is your father?" She remembered him describing Captain Newport that way.

"Not precisely. It's hard to describe the relationship. He is honored like a father."

Two more men joined them. Pocahontas recognized them from her watching days. These were two of the men who never did any work. John Smith introduced them as Misters Ratcliff and Wingfield.

"Come, Smith, did you not give this pretty girl some baubles?" the one called Rat-cliff said.

Pocahontas could see her friend stiffen. Although she did not understand these English words, she felt dismissed by them.

Matachanna and Nokomias came running up. "Nan-taquaus says we need to leave since the days are so short. He does not wish to be on the river at night." Matachanna sounded out of breath.

When Nantaquaus joined them, John Smith introduced them all around.

Rat-cliff left and came back with a basket filled with things. He handed a new hatchet to Nantaquaus. "This is from the King of England as a gift."

John Smith interpreted and continued to tell them what Rat-cliff said as he gave both girls beautiful strings of beads. When he came to Pocahontas, he gave her many strings of beads, a copper bracelet, and a pewter cup.

After everyone thanked the English for the gifts, Nan-taquaus nudged them toward the gate. Pocahontas kept fingering the cold metal of the cup as they said good-bye to all the men.

As they walked toward the gate, John Smith motioned for

them to wait. He ran back to his sleeping lodge and came back to walk with them down to the water.

"Thank you for visiting our village," he said. "And, Pocahontas, thank you for saving my life." He reached inside his vest and pulled out three strings of glistening white beads. "I know you received many gifts today, but this is the gift I planned to give you." He put them over her head.

"Thank you, brother." Pocahontas fingered the beads. "I will treasure them forever."

As they pushed off into the water, Pocahontas looked back and saw a too-thin John Smith watching as they paddled out of sight. She wondered if John Smith's gift would last far longer than the man himself.

9
Saving Jamestown

ell me what you saw," Powhatan said to Nantaquaus and Pocahontas. Flanked by the two of them, he still sat on the edge of his dais. It was a rare moment when all his advisors were gone.

"I spent time studying the cannons," Nantaquaus said. "They are mighty guns and can do much damage, but they would not be useful to us."

Powhatan folded his hands and waited for his son to continue.

"They take too much preparation to fire and then, you only get one massive shot." He shook his head. "With the kinds of attack we face from our enemies—where we never see them coming until they are upon us—these would never work. And if we were to attack, how could we sneak up on them pulling a cannon?"

"You confirm what I have observed, my son. The guns that would benefit us would be the firesticks they carry."

"All this talk about guns and fighting. Aren't we at peace, Father?" Pocahontas hated war talk.

"We are only at peace because our enemies fear us and our friends know our strength." Her father turned to her. "So what did you learn?"

"I sat on a chair." She stopped to describe what a chair looked like. "I had water at a table." Again she used her hands and all her words to describe a table. "And I drank out of a pewter cup." She took out the cup she had been given and put it in her father's hands.

He turned it over and plunked his finger against it. He rubbed his thumb over the embossed decoration. He signaled to Nantaquaus to hand him the bowl with water in it and he poured water into the cup. Putting his mouth on the edge of the cup, he drank all the water.

"Is it not a beautiful thing, Father?"

"Beautiful."

"I want you to have it. It is a cup worthy of a king—no, worthy of the *Mamanatowic*." Pocahontas smiled. How she loved having a gift of worth to give to her great father.

"And how is your English brother?"

Pocahontas sighed. "I fear they starve."

"How can they starve?" Her father dismissed her concern. "I had reports that a ship came. They unloaded enough food to last until planting season, even with the sixty new *tassantassuk* who arrived."

Nantaquaus smiled at Pocahontas.

She shrugged. Why should she be surprised at her father? He always managed to know everything. Well, not everything. "Did your envoy report that seven days after the ship came, a fire burned up most of their lodges and their store-house?"

Now it was her father's turn to be surprised. "A fire? Why did no one tell me?"

"I believe John Smith wishes to keep their weaknesses hidden," Nantaquaus said.

"But if they have no food, they will die." Powhatan sat silently. "Tomorrow, take Rawhunt and Pocahontas and pack as much food as you can fit into your canoe. Take it to my English son. Let him pay us in tools."

"Thank you, Father." Pocahontas put her arms around his neck. "If you could have seen the boy who watched us sip what must have been the last of their rations—he had such hunger in his eyes, but he never said a word."

"Pack a haunch of venison, bear meat, and corn."

Pocahontas could picture how much they could fit into her brother's canoe. It would be enough food to last for two, maybe three weeks.

"Tell John Smith to come to me when he needs more food. We will trade. Tell him to bring his father with him."

This time, as Nantaquaus landed his canoe, both men jumped out and pulled the canoe onto the beach. Pocahontas got out and waited for the shout to announce visitors, but they waited and heard nothing.

Nantaquaus put his hands to his mouth and called, "John Smith!"

The gate opened and their friend came walking out by

himself, rubbing his hands on his breeches. "My friends, I did not know you were coming. I am sorry none were here to greet you. We are trying to rebuild what was lost in the fire."

"We bring food from our father, the great Powhatan," Pocahontas said, smiling.

"This is our uncle Rawhunt, my father's brother. You may have met him at the council." Nantaquaus lifted the haunch of venison out of the boat.

"I remember you. Welcome to our village, Rawhunt." John Smith seemed distracted. "I don't have men to help unload the food right now," he said. "Let me help." He reached in to take the bear meat but seemed to hesitate under the load.

Pocahontas moved as if to help, but Nantaquaus shook his head. John Smith would not want to be seen as weak, especially in front of her father's brother. She reached in and took out a large basket of squash. It looked as good as the day it had been harvested. They kept squash fresh in the storehouse for months under a blanket of straw. Fresh vegetables and berries would help John Smith's people as much as meat and grain.

As they walked into the village few men moved about. Captain Newport came forward to greet them and she could see some of the men John Smith pointed out as newcomers working on the houses. A new storehouse had been constructed close to the cooking pits.

"May I begin to cook a meal while you unload the canoe?" Pocahontas asked.

Her brother looked at her with raised eyebrows. So she had never cooked at home. She'd watched it enough.

"You mix the dough for the *ponepone*," Rawhunt said. "Nantaquaus and I will roast the meat."

The boy Pocahontas remembered came over to watch. She smiled at him, so glad to see that he still lived. "Can you get me water?"

He nodded.

She reached into a small basket and removed three goose eggs. She knew she had to feed close to a hundred men, so she took out another egg. If she could just get the proportions right. She scooped a basketful of dried ground corn and dumped it into the large bowl the boy brought her from the storehouse, adding a good-sized lump of bear fat and the eggs she had cracked. She took a wooden paddle and began to mix it all together. She remembered Alaqua telling them that the pieces of bear fat needed to be no bigger than the pearl threaded through her ear.

Pocahontas tried to picture that pearl as she mixed. When the mixture was crumbly, she poured in water—just enough to make a soft dough. She wondered what the people in her village would think to see their princess cooking like a slave for the English. It felt good, though, like it was important work.

The dough looked just like Alaqua's. She pinched off a piece and put it in her mouth. It tasted the same as well. Her brother and uncle put the venison on a spit over the fire and begin to turn it. It didn't take long for the smell to begin filling the village. Men began to emerge from the shelters to come near and watch. Pocahontas had never seen such hunger among her people.

John Smith joined her. "You saved my life once and you will forever have my gratitude." He inhaled the smells of food. "Now you save the lives of all of our people. England owes you a debt of gratitude as well."

"Not I," she said. "It is my father."

He looked around. "How can I help you?"

"If we were at Werowocomoco, the mothers would now make loaves of *ponepone* and put them into the clay ovens. You do not have ovens here."

"We have iron kettles."

"Iron kettles," she repeated.

"If we put the dough into the kettle over a small fire, the bread will bake slowly as the venison roasts."

They used both kettles, first smearing them with more of the bear fat. Pocahontas divided the dough, shaping each half into a massive loaf on the bottom of a kettle. Soon the smell of baking *ponepone* filled the air, mingling with the rich scent of roasting meat. John Smith poked through the fire, pushing many of the glowing pieces of wood into a pit.

"That lowers the heat so the *ponepone* can bake slowly," he said. "And we'll put the squash into this pit with the ashes so they can roast." He went over to his lodge and brought back two chairs. "With any luck, the food will all be done at the same time and we can feast."

He sat on one of the chairs and motioned to Pocahontas to take the other chair. She smiled but sat on a rock near the fire. "It's much warmer down here."

"If our settlement survives, I wonder if people will remember the little princess who saved us?"

Pocahontas looked down. She didn't know what to say. Her father was the one who saved them. She looked around. One by one, the men and boys had made it out of their lodges

—their houses—lured by the smell of food. She knew the food had come none too soon.

Nantaquaus gestured to her. She knew what that meant.

"We need to leave now," she said to John Smith as she stood to go. "We don't want to have to navigate the river in the dark of night." She didn't mention that they didn't want to take any of the food needed by the English.

"Are you sure you don't want to stay for the feast you've provided?"

"I'm sure."

He walked the three down to Nantaquaus's canoe. He helped them load the tools he had given in exchange for the food. "Thank you, friends."

"You will come to Werowocomoco to trade for more food, won't you?" Pocahontas asked.

"I will come."

"And you'll bring Captain Newport?" she added.

"Your father?" Nantaquaus smiled as he pushed off. He and Rawhunt stabbed their paddles into the water and the boat glided out onto the river.

As they headed back to their village, Pocahontas couldn't help feeling uncomfortable about her father's insistence that John Smith bring Captain Newport to trade at Werowocomoco. Why couldn't they continue to bring the food to Jamestown? Why did he want them in the village?

10
Traitors
and Treachery

$\mathcal{P}$ocahontas knew that the Jamestown party was coming to trade long before it reached the village. That was the thing about having allies all along the route. Runners had been sent ahead from every tribe, warning of the *tassantassuk*.

The last few times the English came, they brought gifts for her father as well as trade goods. Each new meeting showed how little they understood each other. The problem was, her father wanted guns and swords. John Smith was just as determined to keep them out of his hands.

As Pocahontas observed each trading mission, she could see that Captain Newport created problems. John Smith and her father had an understanding of sorts. A grudging respect. The great Powhatan kept trying to outsmart John Smith to get guns and weapons and to strike a better deal for the food the English so badly needed.

But John Smith never seemed desperate. He would work just as hard to get the better end of the deal. And he made sure that her father never got his hand on a single gun or sword.

It had become a game to them, and she could see that her father enjoyed matching wits with John Smith.

But the first time John Smith brought Captain Newport with him the balance shifted. She still remembered the way the captain ignored John Smith and played right into Powhatan's hands.

"Great Powhatan," the captain said, approaching the dais before her father had signaled for him. "I bring gifts."

Her father looked John Smith in the eye before bowing his head to signal that he would accept the captain's gifts.

First the captain pushed forward the boy Pocahontas had seen that first day in Jamestown—the starving boy. "This is Thomas Savage. I've brought him to you to serve you. He will learn your language and help you learn ours."

Pocahontas wondered how Thomas Savage felt about being given as a gift.

The captain then spread out a suit of clothes made with red cloth. One of Powhatan's advisors accepted that on his behalf. Pocahontas could tell that her father was not impressed. Next Captain Newport offered a hat. Another of the men accepted that.

The captain pointed to Thomas Savage and had him go outside. He came back in with a greyhound on a lead. "This dog is for you, Powhatan, sent from England."

Pocahontas could see that this was the gift that delighted her father. He stepped down himself to get the dog, coaxing it up to the dais. The animal curled at his feet. Every few minutes she could see the great Powhatan reach down to stroke the dog's head.

All would have been well if the captain had stepped back and allowed John Smith to trade with her father. Instead the captain laid out an array of tools and pots. Her father offered only a fourth of what he normally gave for each implement. John Smith tried to step in, but Captain Newport would raise his hand to silence the younger man and accept the trade.

"I much prefer trading with your father," Powhatan said, smiling at John Smith.

Pocahontas noticed that her English brother did not translate that comment for the captain. She looked at the amount of grain her father had traded and saw that the English only had a fraction of what they should have received. This could mean another starving time.

John Smith stood behind the captain, saying nothing but fingering several strands of blue beads. Pocahontas recognized the beads as being the same kind as the one Nokomias had given her.

"Will you trade for those beads?" Powhatan asked.

Captain Newport turned around and looked at John Smith, frowning.

"No. These beads are exceedingly rare." He held them so they caught the light streaming in from the open thatch of the roof. "They reflect the very color of the sky above."

Pocahontas could see the trade battle heating up. Her father wanted those beads.

"How much do you want for the beads?"

Captain Newport began to speak up, but this time, John Smith cut him off. "I cannot trade for these beads. I may never be able to replace them. Does the substance from which they are made still exist? I do not know."

Pocahontas fingered the white beads around her neck, subtly letting her father know she'd love to have a few of those sky blue beads adorning her neck.

John Smith smiled. "I see our princess longs for these beads. You know I can deny her nothing since she saved my life."

Powhatan laughed out loud now.

"I will let you have these beads for three hundred bushels of corn—but only because of Pocahontas."

John Smith caught Pocahontas's eye and winked. She knew that had he not worked that barter, their shallop would have headed back to Jamestown nearly empty.

That was not the end of Captain Newport's interference.

At one point he led a whole regiment of men to Werowocomoco to hold an English coronation for Powhatan. They brought the robe and a crown, but the ceremony fell apart when her father refused to kneel to receive the crown. Her father explained that the *Mamanatowic* cannot kneel for anyone. The captain insisted that even their king—the mighty King of England—had to kneel. In the end, Powhatan lowered his head enough for the crown to be placed on him.

It took a dozen men to carry the king's gift to him—a massive carved wooden four-poster bed. When Captain Newport told him it was a gift from the English king, it didn't make the impression he'd hoped. Matachanna looked at it and whispered to Pocahontas that she'd be afraid to sleep on it in case she rolled off into the fire.

No, trading had not gone well.

The worst trade of all came just a couple of days before Captain Newport was to leave in the ship to go back to England.

Powhatan had sent Rawhunt, Nantaquaus, and Pocahontas to Jamestown with twenty turkeys. In exchange they were to get twenty swords.

Pocahontas knew it would never happen. John Smith would not let her father have weapons. She loved her father, but thought John Smith was wise to refuse to trade for weapons if he wanted to ensure the safety of his settlement.

When they arrived, Captain Newport met them at the water. He called for help to unload the turkeys.

"Is John Smith here?" Pocahontas asked.

"No. I sent him with the crew to get one more load of gold to load on the ship."

Nantaquaus looked at Pocahontas. They both knew that the men had found no gold. They were loading the ship with dirt in the hope that in England they could find flecks of the metal somewhere in the pile.

Rawhunt spoke. "Powhatan wishes for twenty swords in exchange for these twenty turkeys."

"Fair enough," Captain Newport said. "Perkins, fetch twenty swords. Wrap them in old linen to protect them."

Pocahontas could not believe it. Twenty swords for twenty turkeys? A turkey was not even worth one fourth of a hatchet.

As they set off for Werowocomoco, the three remained quiet. That trade signaled a fatal change.

"Our father has issued a decree that no one can trade with the English for food until the English are willing to trade guns," Nantaquaus told Pocahontas as they sat mending fishing nets.

"They will starve," Pocahontas said. She still visited Jamestown regularly. Even though she and Matachanna had tried to show them how to plant corn, a combination of salty ground, brackish water, and halfhearted husbandry doomed their efforts.

"They have lived in their village for two planting seasons. Here we are at winter again. When will the English learn to feed themselves?" Nantaquaus's voice revealed his exasperation.

Powhatan's embargo worked. No one would sell the English any food. Another severe starving time set in. Pocahontas could not go to Jamestown now, but she could imagine the desperation.

"Our father has asked John Smith to build him an English house, complete with glazed windows right here in Werowocomoco," Nantaquaus told Pocahontas. "They agreed and sent builders and the finest materials. They have already begun the house."

"A house?" Pocahontas thought that made little sense.

"He also asked for a grindstone, fifty more swords, guns, a rooster and a hen, more *mattassin*, and beads."

"All that for food?"

"Yes. And the runner just announced that John Smith was on his way when his ship became stuck on a sandbar. He's stuck there until high tide."

"Shall we go out and see him?"

"No. Our father no longer trusts John Smith."

Nantaquaus told Pocahontas what they'd learned from the men building Powhatan's English house. Apparently the men preferred living in Werowocomoco to starving in Jamestown. They told Powhatan that John Smith was so desperate because of the embargo that the men planned to show up with guns and take whatever food they needed.

They also told Powhatan all about the defenses in Jamestown, how their guns worked, and how they could keep them from working.

"They are traitors to their own people." Pocahontas couldn't understand why her father would believe them.

"The builders are not Englishmen. They call themselves German. They no longer like the English."

It confused Pocahontas. Trickery and traitors.

"If John Smith and his men make it here to the village, you need to stay away from them."

"Why?" It didn't make sense, but her brother would say no more.

She couldn't stop thinking about her brother's warning. Was some kind of attack being planned? She thought about joining her father in the great lodge, but she didn't want to be part of any kind of attack.

As soon as dusk came, she positioned herself outside the lodge. Because of the opening in the mats for air, she could hear the conversation without being seen. She hoped none of the dogs would sense her and start barking.

Pocahontas heard her father speaking first. "Above all else, we must kill John Smith. Without him, the English will be helpless."

She strained to hear. Had she heard correctly?

"They stay at a lodge near where their ship ran aground."

That must have been her uncle Rawhunt.

"It's simple. John Smith will come to trade tomorrow. He will not offer guns, so we'll send him away. He won't leave without food, so they'll stay the night again, planning to talk trade on the morrow." Powhatan cleared his throat.

Rawhunt took over. "That night, we bring them platters of rich food. While they put down their guns to eat, we attack them."

Pocahontas had heard enough. She slipped away. Not a dog barked and the snow muffled the sound of her movements. She was glad the snow continued to fall. Her footprints would not be seen.

The next morning, she slipped into the great lodge in time to see John Smith trading with her father.

"Why do you come with armed men to my village?" her father was saying. "Are we not family?"

"Why do your men bring bows and arrows to Jamestown when they come?"

"If you want to show you are serious about trading, I demand that you have all your men lay down their arms and come as friends."

"Are we going to talk about trading? I already send my finest builders to work on a house for you." He opened a sack and pulled out a rooster and a hen. "I brought the poultry you requested. These are among the first chickens in the New World."

"This is not a new world," Powhatan said, seizing on John Smith's slip. "This is our old world—our only world."

"I guess there's no sense in looking at the copper and beads I brought?"

"Did you bring weapons?"

This time neither man smiled, and neither seemed to be enjoying the process.

"If you didn't bring weapons, you can leave. I have no corn for you." Powhatan folded his arms across his chest.

John Smith bent to pick up the chickens and put them back into the sack.

"No. Leave the chickens."

John Smith dropped them into the sack. "I'll be back tomorrow."

The storm continued to blow. As soon as darkness fell, Pocahontas wrapped her furs around her and went out to find the lodge near the sandbar. As she knocked on the door, it opened and she faced John Smith.

"Pocahontas. I am so glad to see you." He made a gesture to invite her in.

"No. Listen carefully. My father will have men bring you food tonight. As soon as you put your weapons down to eat, they plan to kill all of you."

"But why?"

"There's no time to talk. I must leave." Pocahontas knew that if her father caught her, it wouldn't matter that she was his favorite daughter. She'd be killed.

"Wait." John Smith went inside and came out with handfuls of beads. "Let me give you something to say thanks."

"Beads." She started crying. "You think I did this for beads? What would my father think if he knew I betrayed him for a few beads?" She began to run toward her sleeping lodge. The snow continued to fall. As she got closer to the village, she saw the men carrying baskets of fragrant food in the direction from which she'd just come.

She didn't sleep that night. The next day she heard that John Smith struck a bargain with her father and sailed home with his boat filled with grain.

All she could think about was her English brother, standing there with strings of beads.

11
Captured

She thought about that night many times over the next four years, and how she never had a chance to say good-bye to John Smith.

It wasn't long after that night that her father made the decision to move the village. It didn't matter that he had the English house he had schemed to get. It didn't matter that Werowocomoco had been home for her entire life. The whole village packed up and moved to Oropax—far away from Jamestown and the English intruders.

She often thought of John Smith. She had wanted him to teach her to make the marks on paper that could be understood by others. She wanted to get on a white bird ship with him and sail across the ocean. She missed talking to him. In John Smith she had found someone who was as curious as she was.

Envoys often brought news of him—his trading missions to other tribes, his exploration of the Chesapeake. One day a messenger came into the new ceremonial lodge at Oropax when Pocahontas was there with her father.

The messenger didn't mince words. "John Smith is dead. They took his body back to his country on a ship."

"He's dead?" Pocahontas could not believe the words he spoke.

"How did he die?" Powhatan asked.

"From the powder they use in their guns."

"Gunpowder? How?" Powhatan seemed shaken.

"They said he was on the small ship they use and he lay down to sleep. He wore that rawhide pouch he always attached to his belt. That's where he kept his gunpowder. Someone on the ship dropped a pipe. A spark from it hit his pouch."

Pocahontas wanted to put her fingers in her ears like she did when she was a little girl and didn't want to hear something.

"It exploded and tore a hole in his side. The men said it tore all the flesh off his middle. The pain was so great, they say he jumped into the river and had to be saved from drowning."

"And he died?" Pocahontas could barely say the words. Her brother. Dead.

"He was still alive when they put him on the ship to England, but he was injured unto death, they said."

Pocahontas left the lodge and never spoke the name John Smith again. Grief wrapped itself around her. She no longer turned somersaults or teased Matachanna or Nantaquaus. She didn't even have any questions left she wanted to ask. But then again, she was no longer eleven years old.

"How good it feels to be away from our village," Pocahontas said as she, Nokomias, and Matachanna splashed in the cool water of the Potomac. The three had been staying with Japazeus, the *weroance* at Passapatanzy. Pocahontas had already seen sixteen summers. It had been more than three summers since she heard about the death of her English brother.

"Look." Matachanna pointed out on the water. "A ship."

"Do you remember the very first time we ever saw an English ship?" Nokomias asked. "Doesn't that seem long ago?"

To Pocahontas it felt like another lifetime.

As the ship drew closer, the girls could see Japazeus running out to meet the ship.

"It's the ship of my friend Captain Argall," the *weroance* said over his shoulder.

The girls hardly paid any attention until the wife of Japazeus came toward them. "I want to see the ship, but Japazeus will not let me go unless I have another woman accompany me."

"I'll go," Matachanna said.

"No, I do not want you," the woman said, wrinkling her nose.

That suited Pocahontas. She didn't trust this woman and would not want Matachanna or Nokomias going with her.

"I want Pocahontas."

"Thank you, but I do not wish to go." Something about this seemed strange.

The woman started crying.

Japazeus, who'd been watching from the ship's deck, came running off the ship. "What did you do to my wife?"

"She doesn't want to come with me," his wife wailed. "I'll never get to see the inside of an English ship." Her crying became louder and louder.

"I'll go," Pocahontas finally said. Surely, stepping onto this ship would be less painful than listening to that woman.

Japazeus's wife clapped her hands, her tears gone as quickly as they came. "Follow me."

Pocahontas climbed up onto the deck and stood there while the woman looked around. *How long will this take?*

Japazeus took Pocahontas over to the captain. "Captain Argall, this is Pocahontas."

She nodded her head in acknowledgment.

Finally, the woman came back to the deck. "Captain, could we sleep aboard ship tonight? I've always wanted to sleep on an English ship."

Pocahontas started to leave.

"I can only let you stay if you are accompanied by another woman."

The woman's claw-like hands grabbed Pocahontas's arm. "Stay, so that I can stay. It's only one night."

The cajoling went on until Pocahontas gave in once again. When she settled onto the sleeping mat below deck she couldn't shake an uncomfortable feeling. Something wasn't right. She woke before dawn and went up to the deck just in time to see Japazeus and his wife leaving. They were thanking the captain for the copper pot and beads they held.

"Where are you going?" Pocahontas tried to follow.

"No. You are to stay here with me." The captain took her by the arm. "I will treat you like a princess, but you are my captive." He pulled her below deck and locked the door of the cabin.

Captive. Her mind went back to the *arakun* caught in the boys' trap. She felt every bit as frantic. She went to the door and began to claw at it. *Stop it. Use your head, not your hands.*

She wondered if her English brother—she still could not say his name—felt this way when Opechancanough captured him. Would there be anyone to set her free?

She lay on the mat and felt the sway of the boat as it got under way. Soon Matachanna and Nokomias would get word to her father. What kind of story would Japazeus tell them?

"Are you awake in there?" Captain Argall's voice shook her out of her daze as he unlocked the door. "Do you want to know why I took you?"

Pocahontas did not speak.

"I am holding you for ransom. I've already sent someone to contact your father." He waited for a response. When none came, he went on. "Do you want to know what you are worth? We're hoping you are worth a boatload of corn, all the English prisoners your father captured, plus all the tools and weapons that your people stole."

Pocahontas still didn't answer. "Well, you are talkative. I guess it's going to be a silent time while we wait to see what you really mean to your father."

And wait they did.

At one point, the captain came in to announce that her father had freed the seven prisoners and sent tools, a few broken guns, and a canoe filled with corn.

"He says he will give another five hundred bushels of corn when we return you, but we're not giving you back until we get every gun back."

With each day, Pocahontas felt more and more frantic. She could not stand confinement. The only way she made it through each day was to remember long rides in Nantaquaus's canoe, cartwheeling across the damp grass, or crossing the footbridge at Werowocomoco. Sometimes she imagined herself falling into the water with a cold splash. Anything to keep from thinking about that locked door.

"Your father doesn't seem like he wants you back." Captain Argall looked almost as antsy as she felt. "We're pulling up anchor and going back to Jamestown. We'll wait him out there."

As the ship got under way once again, she didn't know whether the news was good or bad. She'd be glad to get out of this confinement, but Jamestown? She hadn't been back since that day she made her first *ponepone* for the starving English.

As the ship dropped anchor and she was taken into Jamestown, she realized how much had changed. There was hardly a face she recognized. She even saw two women in the fort. Though this was not the Jamestown of her English brother, she somehow felt as if she'd come home. Why was that?

12
Forever Set Free

Week after week, Pocahontas waited for her father to pay the balance of the ransom and free her. Did the English guns mean more to him than the daughter he always said he loved above all others?

Or had he somehow found out about her betrayal to the English?

After being held aboard the ship, Pocahontas appreciated being free to walk about Jamestown, though she did so without bothering to look up or acknowledge anyone.

One morning as she walked by the large meetinghouse she heard something. She stopped. Had she heard the word *amosens* whispered? She looked around. Was it her father? No, it was not his voice, though it was a voice she recognized. She walked around the building again but heard nothing.

I know that voice.

The next morning she retraced her steps, hoping to hear the voice again. She didn't precisely hear it, but she felt it. She peered inside the building but it was dark. Slipping inside she sat on a bench. She slowly breathed in and out, sensing the word.

"Can I be of help?"

She jumped. How long she had sat with her eyes closed, she could not have said.

"I am Alexander Whitaker, lately of Cambridge." He laughed a self-conscious laugh. "Well that was silly wasn't it, since I'm in Jamestown and you've never been to England."

Something about his manner put her at ease. "I am Pocahontas."

"I know. I've heard the story of your bravery and how you saved the colony from certain death. I wasn't here, but I've heard that when you came bringing food, some kneeled and thanked God for sending an angel."

"An angel? I'm afraid I don't know that word."

"Perhaps now is a good time to speak to you about that." He cleared his throat. "When they first brought you here, they assigned me the task of helping you polish your English and teaching you to read and write, but I didn't want to bother you right away."

Pocahontas didn't understand what he was saying.

"Read and write. You know—" He took out a goose quill and began to make scratches on the paper.

"That's write? I want to learn to write." She looked at the paper. "What is read?"

"Read is when you can look at these words and know what they mean. Do you know what this word says?"

She looked long at the word. She couldn't see any pictures or symbols to give it away. "No, I do not know."

"It says Pocahontas."

She touched the word with her fingers.

"See. Each of these letters is a symbol for a sound. This one——" He put the paper in her hands and pointed to the symbol nearest the hand she did not use as much as the other. "This one is a p. It sounds like this." He put his lips together and made soft "puh" sounds.

"So that is how it works. You break down the word into sounds. I always wondered how it worked."

He took the paper from her hands. "I didn't approach you before this because . . . well, because you seemed to be in a world of your own. I didn't know what to say to you."

She didn't answer.

"I like not that you've been captured." His voice became firmer. "I do not understand the wisdom of it. It feels like a travesty."

"I do not understand all you say, but thank you for that."

"What made you decide to come into our church today?"

"Church?" She turned that word around her tongue and wondered how one would write a "ch." She looked around the building. "When I walked by the church yesterday I heard the voice call *amosens*. I came back today to see if I heard that voice again."

"Did you? I mean hear the voice."

"No, I didn't hear the voice say *amosens*, but I sensed the voice in here."

"What does *amosens* mean?"

"In English, you say *daughter*."

"Have you ever heard this voice before?"

Pocahontas laughed. It was the first time she'd laughed in a long time. "You ask as many questions as I used to."

"Used to?"

Pocahontas paused to think about that. "When I was smaller all I ever did was run, jump, turn somersaults, and ask questions. My father loved that about me. It irritated others." She laughed. "I wanted to know everything."

"When did that change?"

Again Pocahontas had to stop. "I don't know. Maybe it was when someone I loved died. Or maybe it was when I betrayed someone I love very much."

Alexander Whitaker nodded his head. "Those can be devastating. Let's talk more about those if we continue to meet."

"I'd like to continue to meet. I want to learn to write. And to read."

He smiled. "Then meet we will. But back to my earlier question—have you ever heard that voice before?"

"I have. Twice. Both times the voice—the person—invited me to seek Him, to know Him better."

"Do you know whose voice it is?"

"I believe it is the voice of *Gitchee Manitou*—the Great Spirit."

"You did not think it Okeus, your Powhatan god?"

"No, I knew it was not Okeus. This voice was filled with love for me. Like a father for his daughter." As soon as she said it, she put her hand over her mouth.

"Are you angry at your father for not ransoming you?"

"Yes." She stopped. "No." She looked at the man. "Can I speak to you true?"

"Did you know that anything said to me is secret? Because I am a minister, you can tell me anything and I shall never repeat it."

"A minister. I do not know that word."

"This is the house we have made to worship God—the one you call *Gitchee Manitou*. I am the one who cares for God's house and God's people."

"Then let me tell you about my father." And she began to tell him about the great Powhatan. How he loved his daughter, but how he also had to work the best barter deal he could work. How he loved his people and wanted peace and yet would plot to capture and kill a whole nation. How he could adopt an Englishman as his own son and later order him killed. "I fear I don't even know my father. Is he wise and good, or is he cunning and treacherous?"

"For most of us, the truth probably lies somewhere between the two possibilities. We battle between what we long to be and what we fall back into."

He took an object off the shelf. It was covered in skin, but inside it had leaves of thinnest paper. "This is the Bible. Have you heard of it?"

"No."

"This is what I'll use to teach you to read. It is a book of God's Word."

"*Gitchee Manitou*'s words are in there?"

"Yes."

"I want to hear them."

"Let me read a passage from His Word. It was written by one of His servants, Paul. 'For the good that I would, I do not: but the evil which I would not, that I do.'"

Pocahontas thought about that. "Yes. Those words are wise. We want to do good and we end up being evil."

"We talked about your father's battle between good and evil. What about you?"

Pocahontas put her hands up to her heart and hunched over. "I betrayed my father."

"I think I know when this happened, but tell me anyway."

"My father planned to kill a group of the English. I heard about it and warned them. They were on their guard and escaped death."

"So was it a good thing you did or a bad thing?"

"It was both. I am glad I saved the lives of those men, but I betrayed my father and my people."

"Does it bother you?"

"Every day."

"And you cannot go to your father and ask his forgiveness?"

"No. Too many people would pay with their lives. The person who left the mat open on the lodge so I could hear. The person who should have been guarding the house where the men stayed. The mothers who did not know I slipped out."

"But you feel a need for forgiveness?"

"More than anything."

Alexander Whitaker talked to her about forgiveness—how much people need it to be free. And about how God—*Gitchee Manitou*—sent His Son to take away those sins.

"What do I need to do?"

"Talk to Him. Ask Him to forgive you. That's it. You'll know." He stood up. "Let me go so you can talk to Him. Can we meet here every morning? We'll talk and I'll teach you to read and write."

Her face lit up. "Yes. I will be here."

After he left she sat and thought about what he said. *Talk to Him*, Alexander Whitaker had said. "I have sinned against my father and against my people." She was quiet, listening. She didn't hear a voice, but she sensed a listening. "Will You forgive me even if I can't ask my father to forgive?"

She didn't hear anything, but she felt a lightness she hadn't felt after that night when John Smith held out a handful of beads.

"I want to be Your child. Is that why You whispered *amosens* all those years ago?"

She didn't hear any voice, but she found a laughter bubbling up inside of her. "That was a question, wasn't it? Are You giving me back my questions?" She wondered if He would be sorry. She already felt hundreds of questions forming inside. She picked up the Bible that the minister had left. Were some of the answers in here?

Why did it take having to become a captive before she could know what it meant to be free?

Oh, she had questions.

Epilogue

Pocahontas's story did not end with her captivity and the freedom she found in the living God, *Gitchee Manitou*, and His Son, Jesus Christ. Her father never did ransom her, although he sent Nantaquaus to make certain she was treated well. She continued to learn to read and write and to study the Bible. After a year or two with the English, she asked to be baptized. Her name was changed to Rebecca and everyone called her Lady Rebecca in honor of her royal status. She adopted English dress, including corsets, crinolines, farthingales, and pointy leather shoes.

As she grew in her faith and her understanding of the English language, she also grew to love one of the settlers. John Rolfe had become the most successful planter in the colony. He was fair and honest, a hard worker, respected by everyone. He had come to love Pocahontas as he watched the way she served his people and served his Lord. They married in Jamestown on a beautiful spring day in April 1614.

A child, Thomas, was born to them a little more than a year later. Pocahontas loved her life—a beautiful home, a loving husband, and a precious baby.

Remember when she first sighted the white bird boats of the English? How she longed to sail across the ocean on one? Her dream came true when her baby, Thomas, was only a year old. The men of the Virginia Company asked her to come to England to meet Queen Anne. Pocahontas, her husband John Rolfe, and the baby sailed across the Atlantic and landed at Plymouth in 1616. Matachanna accompanied her to help care for Thomas.

By all accounts, her stay in London was a social success. The Lady De La Ware took Pocahontas under her wing and escorted her to balls and dinners and audiences with important people. Londoners first came to see her because she was a Powhatan and a princess, which sounded foreign and exciting. After they met her, though, they continued to seek her out because of her gentle, accepting manner. She was presented at court in an elegant court gown and hat and afterward had her portrait painted.

John Smith had not died, as had been reported to Pocahontas. He managed to survive his trip to England. Pocahontas was surprised by a brief meeting with him in London. Too brief, however, to recapture that old comfortable friendship.

Perhaps the whirl of parties became too much for the young mother. Perhaps the damp London climate took its toll. No one knows for sure, but Pocahontas fell ill on board the ship, waiting for the wind to come up that would carry her family home to America.

Her husband knew she was too sick to sail, so he had the

captain dock the ship at Gravesend. He moved Pocahontas and baby Thomas to an inn close by.

It soon became apparent that Pocahontas would not be making the trip back to her country. The little girl who once turned somersaults in the lodge of one of the most powerful men in the New World turned to her husband as she took her last breaths and said, "All must die. It is enough that the child lives."

At her funeral, they read the words of her Lord from John 11: "I am the resurrection, and the life: he that believeth in me, though he were dead, yet shall he live."

The story of Pocahontas laying down her life for that of John Smith has become the stuff of legends, but perhaps even more important is the knowledge that the young princess saved the struggling colony from starvation. Her bravery helped birth a new nation.

Glossary of Powhatan Words

Note: Most of the Powhatan language has been lost. John Smith, who recorded much of what we do know, often spelled the same word differently at different times, so alternate spellings can be found.

Amosens. Daughter.
Apasoum. Opossum. A word we get from the Powhatan.
Apooke. Indian tobacco.
Arakun. Raccoon—this is where we get our word *raccoon*.
Cattapeuk. Spring.
Cohattayough. Summer.
Espaniuks. Spanish people.
Gitchee Manitou. The God of creation, literally, the Great Spirit.
Huskanaw. The ceremony in which boys move from childhood into manhood.
Maraowanchesso. Boy.

Mattassin. Copper.

Nepinough. The time of ears of corn forming—a season between spring and summer.

Okeus. The fearsome god believed by the Powhatans to govern the affairs of earth.

Pemmenaw. Thread made of grass fibers.

Ponepone. Cornbread.

Popanow. Winter.

Quintans. A dugout canoe.

Quintansuk. (Plural) Canoes.

Quiyoughsokuk. Medicine men or wise men.

Roanoke. Shells used for beads.

Suckhanna. Water.

Taquitock. Fall (autumn).

Tassantassa. A stranger or an outsider.

Tassantassuk. (Plural) Outsiders.

Waugh! Exclamation, pronounced "wow!" Linguists believe it is from the Powhatans that we get our exclamation, wow!

Weghshaughes. Meat.

Weroance. Local chief.

Proper Names

Note: Except for those characters noted as fictional, all these characters come from the pages of history.

Alaqua. Fictional woman who added Nokomias to her family.

Japazeus. Local *weroance* of the Patawomecks at the village of Passapatanzy.

Mamanatowic. Paramount chief, greatest one—title of Powhatan, Pocahontas's father.

Matachanna. Pocahontas's younger half-sister.

Nantaquaus. Pocahontas's older half-brother, also sometime referred to in Smith's writings as Nantaquoud or Naukaquawis.

Nauiraus. Appomattoc man who worked as a guide/language teacher to the English.

Nokomias. Fictional Chesapeake captive who becomes Pocahontas's friend.

Pocahontas
    aka **Amonute** and **Matoaka**

Powhatan. Name of the people, but also name of the ruler of the federation of Powhatan people and name of a village as well.

Opechancanough. Powhatan's younger, more aggressive brother.

Rawhunt. Powhatan's elderly trusted advisor and older brother.

Wahunsunakuk. Powhatan's given name.

Place/Tribe Names

𝒩ote: The names of tribes, chiefs, and places can be confusing because they often shared the same name.

Chesapeake. The name of the tribe that Powhatan massacred just before the English landed. Many believe the last survivors of the Roanoke Colony—the "lost colony"—had been part of this tribe. Chesapeake is also the name of the bay and the region surrounding it.

Chickhominy River. A tributary of the James River.

Pamunkey River. Now called the York River.

Paspahegh. The village and people nearest Jamestown. The Jamestown settlement was built on Paspahegh lands.

Passapatanzy. A village of the Patawomeck people.

Patawomeck. An independent tribe, not part of the Tsenacomoco, but connected with Powhatans, on the Patawomeck River.

Patawomeck River. Now called the Potomac River.

Powhatan. A village on the Powhatan River near the falls. Parahunt, one of Powhatan's sons, was *weroance* at Powhatan. Pocahontas and the leaders of the Powhatan nation did not live at Powhatan but at Werowocomoco.

Powhatan River. Now called the James River.

Rasawrack. The camp where John Smith was taken after being captured. Rasawrack was also the name of the faraway main town of the Monacans—enemies of the Powhatans.

Tsenacomoco. The federation of nations united by Powhatan covering 8,000 square miles and about 14,000 people.

Werowocomoco. Pocahontas's village—the seat of power for her father's federation.

Daughters of the Faith Series

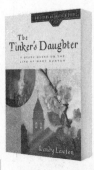

Imagine meeting someone famous before she was famous. This biography series about the lives of some well-known Christian women when they were young girls allows for just such an experience. Read about the adventurous early lives of Underground Railroad pioneer Harriet Tubman; Mary Bunyan, whose father wrote Pilgrim's Progress; Mary Chilton, who came to America on the Mayflower; and more.

Courage to Run
ISBN-13: 978-0-8024-4098-3
The Tinker's Daughter
ISBN-13: 978-0-8024-4099-0
Almost Home
ISBN-13: 978-0-8024-3637-5
Ransom's Mark
ISBN-13: 978-0-8024-3638-2
The Hallelujah Lass
ISBN-13: 978-0-8024-4073-0
Shadow of His Hand
ISBN-13: 978-0-8024-4074-7

by Wendy Lawton
Find it now at your favorite local or online bookstore.

www.MoodyPublishers.com

Max & Me Mysteries Series

ISBN-13: 978-0-8024-6253-4

ISBN-13: 978-0-8024-6254-1

ISBN-13: 978-0-8024-6255-8

Bestselling author Patricia H. Rushford begins a new mystery series for middle grade readers, set in the Cascade Mountains of Washington. Max Hunter and Jessie Miller are unlikely best friends. Both girls are 12 years old; Max is wild and independent, Jessie is calm and thoughtful. Both have secrets: Max has a troubled home life she tries to keep well-hidden; Jessie is fighting leukemia. But they look after each other and form a deep and abiding friendship that carries them through life when everything falls apart.

by Patricia H. Rushford
Find it now at your favorite local or online bookstore.

www.MoodyPublishers.com